A Sky Held Captive

Poetry and Short Fiction

Timothy Chrisman

authorHOUSE®

AuthorHouse™
1663 Liberty Drive
Bloomington, IN 47403
www.authorhouse.com
Phone: 1 (800) 839-8640

Cover design by Brenda Nemeth

Published by AuthorHouse   04/12/2017

ISBN: 978-1-5246-8626-0 (sc)
ISBN: 978-1-5246-8624-6 (hc)
ISBN: 978-1-5246-8625-3 (e)

Library of Congress Control Number: 2017905285

Print information available on the last page.

This book is printed on acid-free paper.

For My Wife, Robin,
Without whom......

Contents

Prairie

Two millenia, nearly, after a coming of their Christ
came the fathers to their foundling.

Looking at forests unknown to their fathers' lands
they cut away the trees to reveal
naked houses and planted fields and travel-worn roads
to carry them to hidden cities.

And on their lands and in their cities grew
towering crops and fattened children and an appetite
for restlessness.

They came to a prairie, verdant and burnt,
with no existence before a white man's living memory,
to a landscape unpeopled to their eyes,
and declared it good enough
for a man to stretch his legs and build some things

M-Squared

A May afternoon, your new home, though a stranger's house to me,
A Chinese figurine, I forget who you said gave it to you,
stared at me over your shoulder, from behind your ashed face.
As we whispered the end of our two-year silences
Who could know that when we finally spoke again we would voice such brutish words
Like chemo or metastasize or stage four, or that
Your old jokes about bad hair days would come to mean curled clumps
Falling in sorrowing shimmers on sterile floors?

A last embrace before a dying.
I won't come to your funeral, I said, don't ask that of me.
But I knew your never would, because, though you sought
a thousand answers of me over those many years,
you always held back, ever stilled your tongue,
despite your heart's nudging entreaties, from seeking the hardest one.
Which reply, I wondered and wonder still, did you fear hearing?

Word of your death came to me heralded by a mournful ping,
one more cc: on a list of thirty, saying everyone's best friend was gone.
Was my conceit any less than twenty-nine others in thinking
that you wouldhave meant that particular message only to me.

Do you know (thanks to her I now think you might) that
I banished your song, hid away that melody, for over a year?
But, now and then, I take it out in melancholy tribute
On blurred nights, with a raised glass of rum toast on a minds-eye lanai.

And that light, the one we spoke of, the one about which our poet sang.
Are you pleased to know I think I see it now?
I first glimpsed its glow as another May day slipped into night and another fresh day.
Somehow (again due to her) I think you are?

I wish for you serenity, old friend.
May you now bask in the peace
of that light that glowed beyond your woods.

Report to the Indian Commissioner:
The Ballad of Capt. Fallleaf

I let you know when I was under Col. Sumner
It was five years ago
We went out west
It was on the big river,
on the headwaters.

We found the chyanne Indians.
Two days and a half we tracked them,
After the battle
We got to the Indian town.
There was nobody there
All souls were gone.
We commenced to the burning
to burn all that was there
Even the meat
We burned it all to ashes.

We made tracks.
After that in five days
We came to Arkansas.
Then after that I asked Col. Sumner,
To let me go home.
He said "you can go home.
I shall let you go home"

Next day, I started.
Two days I traveled with the mail.
Then I got home.
I went to the fort.
I went to the quartermaster.
I brought him a letter,
From Col. Sumner.

I was payd.
He payd me 350 dollars.
He payd me in gold.
I was well satisfied.

And I was glad,
For we had gained the battle.
I brought one scalp.
I killed the man myself.
And my people came
To see the scalp.
They gathered around for to dance,
And for to make merry,
For as is our role

Before I left Col. Sumner
he gave me a promise of land,
but I have not yet received it.
No, not yet.

One year after I was under Major sedgewick.
It was then the Kiowa Indians.
There then was a brave man.
Settank was his name.
He was a wild Indian.
We found him near fort Bent.
We run him 30 miles,
him and his women and children.
He run out from his people,
And got away.
The prisoners that we took,
we brought them to Fort Bent,
in Arkansas.
Then we went away,
went to Pawnee Fork.

There I told Major Sedgewick,
"I want to go home."
He said, "Go home."

I arrived there,
and the next day I went to the fort,
to the quartermaster.
I got my pay.
I got it all in gold,
but land I was promised,
that I have not got yet.

I got word from my old friend General Fremont.
He wanted my service.
I found him in Springfield,
In Mo.
But not long could I stay with him.
He was called to the east.
He paid me before he went.
Land I was promised,
but had not got yet.
And the money I have not got yet,
neither I,
nor my men.

After one year I went to the south,
in the army.
I was told to do so.
I have done as the government wanted.
I had 85 men with me.
I called them my own men.
Near Fort Gibson we saw the Choctaw,
the halfbreed.

We played ball with them.
50 we laid on the ground.
60 we took prisoner,
even the Choctaw General,
him I took myself alone.
He was a big sesesh;
100 union men he had killed.
I brought him to the Cherokee.
They killed him.
They gave him no time to live.

After that we started homeward;
We went near Fort Scott.
Then I said to Col. Bridges,
"I want to see my people."
He gave me furlough,
15 days.

After the 15 days were gone,
and after 8 days back in the command,
I was taken sick.
While I was laying sick,
Col. Bridges was put to prison by other officers;
the whole command was removed,
and I was left sick in the camp.

6 days after that,
I was trying to go home with 6 of my men.
I thought sick man no good to the government.
But 3 days after
all of my men came home,
without me,
they understood not the command of whites.

We tried to please the government,
the best way we could.
I thought I had done my duty.
We look for he government to pay us;
we look for it as soon as possible,
for we are in need of money.
I look for an answer soon.

Yr obdt servant

Connecticut Dance

Another life lived on the surface
in minimalist Connecticut.

More cultured conversations without words
above the mannered cutlery.

Another dancer refusing the invitation,
strength ebbed by timidity.

One more languid summer at the Vineyard
after a Rite of Spring.

Another existence within the hardened bounds of privilege,
a choreography of waste.

Comes the Snow

A hungry wistfulness falls with the diamonding snow,
lowering the sky,
all trees become birches.
Midnight shadows the day,
softening the jagged edges,
leveling the thoughts
The quiet, oh the sweet sweet sweet quiet
that encircles, folds itself upon the hidden earth,
a consummation to the man who enjoys feeling oneness

Chalkdusted By A Fleeing Moon

Somewhere on the desultory path from Dreamgiver
to cuckold in quick decline
was revealed a messiah no longer wishing
the burden of belief

Tired, irrevocably fatigued, from the attacks
upon a fortress of silence,
built upon brick after brick of indifference,
he left upon that dream-escape holiday,
forgetting entirely the conversations
consummated on soft, hilled ground
chalkdusted by a fleeing moon.

Marching across newly fallow fields,
guarded by cornstalk sentinels standing a mute watch,
the supplicants robe was cast off,
a recusant no more.

A Hellene's Children In the Province Of Adams

So far was it from his,
he had taken to imagining that world,
her people, her place.
New England, privileged, pillared now, but
not old stock, interlopers.
Names and features crying ethnic, other-regional,
not US.
Perhaps swarthy, with a taint of the green, warm sea.

But how quickly the foreign children
found their places to take.
Attitudes sponged, lips hardened, that look acquired.
Music lessons, dance, every hour filled
at a mother's demand.
Many, many, many blessings invoked,
gratitude required.

White-spired Congregationalist churches,
dinner parties of Prokofiev and portfolios.
Private, same-faced schools
of competing plaids
of wool and Indian cottons,
where bells tolled for holidays spent
roaming snowed hills,
memories idyllic.

Updike, he thought.
Yes, ... Updike.
Have you read Updike, he asked of her?
Did you live that Mapled world,
recognize that sense of place?.

The Conestoga Cigar Store and Snooker Parlour

A blue-painted relic,
only vaguely aware of its role as a living anachronism,
The Conestoga Cigar Store and Snooker Parlour remains
cool and dark and many-shadowed no matter the season,
offering its cloistered refuge to a discerning clientele.

Among the commodities bought and sold,
on the list of things borrowed and bartered
within its mirrored wall, through it swirls of smoke,
in earshot of touting voices, beneath winked eyes,
were bootleg whiskey and a sportsman's intuition,
and a man's vote or a woman's sloping breasts.

Burrowing

Burrowing, down, down, deeper still
I have fallen within myself
Burrowing, dark, dark, blacker still
Searching for the elusive core.

Above a shaft's lip
Peering over, looking, seeking
So many eyes searching for me
A light haloes over their heads, faint, so faint, fainter still,
As if a twenty-four hour night is about to descend

Amalia

A first sense of her
not yet sure, but surmised
was that
nearly every one of her sentences
was many layered, leveled, limbed.

"A minefield?"
one friend offered as metaphor.

No, no, in reply, not quite that;
a cool, blue pack of ice,
berged, barbed, beautiful when revealed,
dangerous when unsuspected.

"And does she mean harm?"
again the friend.
"Is she .... ?"

Never, not malicious, surely,
not a malevolent, stinging thing
awaiting a prey too innocent for survival;
she offered her self as enticement only to those
unafraid of the depths.

Amalia Swimming Against The Yule Tide

Tightly around her is drawn the Hebrew cloak,
a comforter, a badge,
shield at times;
also to her
a banner held fiercely aloft
signalling a fortress to be defended
against burrowers of her own kind;
traitors to a cause holy, sacred, ancient,
and deserted much too often;
unfurled at old enemies,
darkening still her horizon;
opponents drawn bull-like to its blood-libeled field
rampant with a tongue of shtetl-fire flame and
twisted wire scarred across
a Lenten-palsied, clinched, Viennese fist
sated only by the face of Hebrew descent.

For the first time deep brown eyes
see me among the villain brigade.
Twisting, tallying, ashen fingers
count me with the unrighteous.
There is no such truth,
though now she will not see,
I am no enemy of hers,
of her kind.

They Put My Little Girl in a Cage

They put my little girl in a cage today.
Oh I know it is a pretty green tent around her hospital bed,
meant to protect her and others till this darkening storm passes,
only a precaution, best for all concerned,
but she and I know,
they put her in a cage.

"Daddy, I want my life back,"
her contorted little body against the tent.
Trying to hold hands through the net,
like prisoner and visitor,
forehead to forehead.
"Dad, I think about you all the time,
even when I am on vacation."

On the phone,
"Dad, they crated me in this cage again."
"I know, baby."
"Come get me out, dad."
"I am sorry, baby."

What sort of HellWorld is this?
Where protein, giver of life,
can kill a little girl?"

And to think some
some still screed from the top of their diseased minds,
that a just and loving god exists
Dumb fucks,
One and all.

Crusaders

Crusaders, gird in silvery metal boxes,
wrought by the blacksmith's fiery forge,
seek to slay the Muslim heart, bleed the soul.
Fucking, Christian fanatics,
ardour fueled by Pope Urban's infamy.
Did they know what they were begetting?

New crusaders
strap on the Nobel-invented raiment
Scream your blood-filled screed,
Who will you kill today?
My wife?
My little girl?

You religion-seduced assassins.
Take yourself to an arid, feckless desert.
Immolate yourself.
Let the flames rise in the void.

Decades

First

My uncles hid their condoms in my bedroom,
in the wall behind loose fleur-di-lis wallpaper, in a space unartfully carved
in the plasterboard,
next to my picture of Mickey Mantle (the Mick chasing down a ball in
deep left-center)
I thought it was bubble gum, wondered why they refused to share.
Uncle Danny, last-born, second-dead after a short stilted life of unfocused,
unintended anger,
humming a song about de-flavored chewing gum, steals into the room
lips to mouth,
eyes in a showman's wink that bespoke saying nothing to grandma, slips
me a quarter
and departs with a decidedly-danceful step.

Trickles of blood on a rusty, black Ford's fender,
in a schoolyard of cinders and embarrassed grass, hard by pile of red bricks
gone to brown,
squalls of tears, squawks of heaving interrupted sobs from a scrunched
first-grade face,
compelling evidence, Milord, of the dangers of crack the-whip and weak hands.
Epithets, menacings, revenges loud and avowed, fisted punishments awaiting,
one-hundred steps to the guilty's-gallows, slow steady, inexorable, the final tolling,
thoughts of deliverance, divine intervention mere curling wisps too
unsubstantial to court,
assured fate a beckoning curled finger, but across the street, waiting,
smiling, stands hope.
Grandpa's sandpaper hand takes mine, my stride matches his as we head home.

Mom holding me,
sitting on the roof of Grandma and Grandpa's half-buried house on McIlroy Avenue.
God, isn't she so thin, plaid blouse, rolled-up jeans obscure those skinny legs
(her unheld great-granddaughter Lyndsay has those legs, bless her),
looking not out at the world (like me, she was not good having her photo taken),
but at me.
A memory, hell, I was what two, three?
No, a grainy black and white etched on my soul.

A cowboy in a three -piece brown tweed suit and a tweed cap
("I don't know how your mom did it, but she always dressed you like a little prince."),
sitting on a mechanical pony in Schultz's bargain basement.
Mom slips in a nickel, smiles, tells me to hold on tight.
A story to tell Gramps about riding across my Texas ranch.

Second

Even a nine-year old didn't need Eric Severeid to tell him on Sunday
that Bull Conner was a redneck, trogdolytic prick,
or that fevered dogs should not feast on Black flesh,
or that Birmingham in 1963 was a cesspool Gomorrah of hatred and filth.
I was smarter than that.

The Waterman's Daughter

The waterman's daughter
ever smells the sea.
And smiles at the memory of a man
lathering his face with brush and cup.

He waterman's daughter
hears the music in everyone.
And stands willing to accept
their song as sung.

The waterman's daughter
Seeks the perfect purse.
And fills it with lists
Of other people's wishes.

The waterman's daughter
makes a home for everyone.
And fills it with pillows and chocolate
for the comfort of all.

The waterman's daughter
swallows a wretching cough.
And know it is a sure harbinger
of her return to the sea.

Deities Must Be Argued With

Beneath eyes of a pontifical caste,
lips twisted into an ecclesiastical smile, he sneered,
"One man's bridge is another man's scaffold."
Arrogant bastard, feckless user of the uncomprehending,
toyer of those without courage to question,
profferer of poofery, slights of mind, and legerdemain,
haranguer of the hopelessly frightened, sophist to the stupid,
egomaniacal enabler of those unbekannt of enigma,
perverse, peripatetic purveyor of mushed pablum,
who do you imagine yourself to be?

Doors

Corridors, halls, passageways beckon me forward.
Caged lights above, dangling, dim, limning Hopper shadowscapes.
Christ, why are lights never bright these days,
no longer incandescent, almost never illuminating.

Doors, doors, doors, infinite doors,
cul de sacs of wood and varnish, rows, rows, brigades of them,
unending, unnumbered, though perhaps dated, epoched.
Which to open, which to avoid, which will haunt, which will succor?

Vouchsafed Dreams

We all have our dreams, Martin.
Not as grand, surely, as yours,
but have them we do, and we
hold some just as sacred.
And sometimes, no matter the purchase
they so tightly have on our souls,
even the selfish among us will
let them sputter and dim, go quietly away
so that others may realize theirs,
even though the sweet agonies of martyrdom
holds no allure.

When You Sleep

For My Daughter Brynn. Who never lets Autism define her

Who are you in your sleep, little girl?
I wondered that tonight when I peeked in
and your star nightlight revealed a face at peace
with a strand of hair across your nose.
and your devoted Hank on guard at your feet.
Sweet is much too inadequate a word for it,
too parsimonious, incredibly meager
Please let it be you, the one I know
That is enough,
for you
for both of us.
For the world does not ken you, nor you it.

What is the world in which you sleep, little girl?
That waking, half-walled world that cannot quite see you
and which you struggle to peer onto, never quite clearly,
the world you strain and rage and kick to join
And you are opaque to it,
Why cannot it see you as we do?
Never mind, forget it, let it go.
Our world is better, truer.
Our world is us
Foreheads touching
Fingers interlaced
A kiss before you fall asleep into your world.

Gedankenlos

I, coveter of rogue thought,
examiner of lives through a jeweler's loupe,
filterer of evolving emotions through a much-faceted prism,
sometime intrepid diver into tossing seas,
parser of each syllable, spoken or merely contemplated,
have willed to myself to a time of unthinkingness,
testated onto myself a surcease of feelingness,
steered me to sail becalmed shoal-less shores.
The result?
We'll see

Einsatzgruppen

Lightning graces the shoulders
of drunken, tho well-trained arsonists.
Orders are orders.
Duty is duty.
So says the gruppenfuhrer.

Judenfrei is our mission.
How quickly jews burn,
a little gasoline and timbers
from tight packed Latvian forests..

Flesh feeds the eternal flames.
Orders are orders,
It is you are me.

Do not the flames purify?
Does not the incendiary match
Change worlds with its flicker?

You tell me,
are you not the other?
Will you not betray me?
Betray the Fatherland?
Inject your poison into
my purer blood?
Taint me and mine for generations?

Orders are orders, duty is duty.
I obey.

Chrisman

Taking back the name
I was born with.
No more flying a false flag,
one I could not honor.

My name was taken away at seven,
another forced upon me.
I never asked for it.
It just appeared,
And so teachers called me
By the strange new name,
but I always knew who I was.

Pyrrhic

The night often ends in sadness;
Blood trails on my head.
Robin noted it.
Very tall men and doors
often come into conflict.
Also wars within me,
No victors emerge,
no clear cut winner.
Stalemate at best;
stalemate beats loss,
both sides declare victory,
Pyrrhic or not.

Scattered Dream Ill-Recollected

In dreams scattered and ill-recollected, My grandfather begat the apocalypse, Then he held my hand as the sky lowered to touching range and the sky, the sky, the sky, gave forth to streams of lights, wicked, towering lights, like fireworks, or missile strikes in video games, or lightning bolts aiming for certain things or peoples, perhaps sinners, maybe saints. He held my hand through all, smoke, haze, redemption, sainthood, sins original and aped, Dante paused over his pen, pondering an eighth circle,
Torquemada with his piggish smile painting, the earth in scarlet red. My grandfather held my hand. I was not frightened

Sorrows of the Selfish

The sorrow of the selfish, though pitiable and deserved,
eviscerates the soul no less than the sadness of the saint.
Mean and self-inflicted and of an unholy ugliness it may be,
it still cuts, slices, burrows into the self-flagellated flesh.
It is its own Torquemada salting scar-red, self-hewn wounds,
but its own-hand-lit auto-da-fe burns no less fierce
than the winged, rapier-thrust flames enrobing the martyr.

The Amazin' Skateboarding Jesus

Spring in the city of the entitled,
Plumed, scabbarded, solemn men march past,
Just the right tone of mourning,
Just the exact set of the jaw to show piety and service,
Panis Angelicus sung on key and with just the proper lilt,
One more soul consigned to a restful place all are told,
Solemn, aching, but resolute and comforted widow's eyes pass by.
But then, as usual, cloying, absurdity rises
Look up. Look up, nudge the person beside you to look up.
Bronzed, shiny broken Jesus speckles just up there, glistens down,
Formulaic, but broken, a crucifix segmented and missing pieces.
Christ weaving through traffic, a crown of a do-rag instead of thorns,
The Amazing Skateboarding Jesus Christ, Saviour of all believers, mocks us.

Souls Uncoupled

The uncoupling of souls,
once loving, amorphous, without bounds,
takes place on moonless, bereft, silent nights
racked with scudding, writhing, heartless winds
so eerie they seem scarlet-eyed and nearly visible,
accompanied by the dissonant note of a mute sob.

Rankean Villainy

I hate scurrying time,
despise its need to move on.
Ranke's moving river of history frustrates me to screams
I want to capture it,
make it my liege,
in something other than memory.

Cicada Nights

On these tightening nights the cicada's song seems to rise
to drown out my strangled voice,
Or perhaps I am whispering so low so
you cannot hear my thoughts kindle and smolder.
Thoughts, you must realize, are not doubts, ponderings not discontent.
Remember that.

How you hate my melancholy, this I know
You take it upon your shoulders, evidence of some negligence or fault,
But it is mine alone, long simmering, always there, before you.
Wrought within me, fashioned out of my peculiar parts by my uncraftsmen-
like hands.
I am its maker, never, ever you
You are not to blame, never the cause.
Remember that.

Lyndsey Sue

Your little voice,
how I love the sound of a three-year old talking,
fills a Christmas living room.
You playfully bit Aunt Robin's belly.
No malice intended.

What a delicate face you show to the world.
Those pretty blonde curls.
That tiny cupid mouth.
That hipless, skinny little body
Revealed by your 60s' hippy girl jeans.

Beautiful three-year olds should not have
ugly time bombs ticking silently in their bird-like chests,
should not inherit a family's curse.
I watched you playing,
dancing with your singing Barbie doll.
It broke my heart

Birkenau

In Birkenau,
voices still call out;
soft, murmuring echoes return
borne upon a wind of years;
not cries of agony, nor shrieks of degradation,
but muted reverberations of pain
eloquent for the want of words.

In this place
visions shimmer, taunt, beckon,
like a parched man's dreams
and look upon the trespasser with grey chasms
in the place of eyes.

Here, in this place, here,
man descended into beast;
the blooded animal was exalted
the Seraphim averted their gaze.

Vanity

Onto a street muted by a chemise-filtered sunlight
steps the woman whose only desire
is to be coveted.
Led by a harnessed team
of three dogs well-bred and yipping, she prances
through the foretaste of a still distant season.

Each stranger with male eyes causes
her pace to slow, measurably, just a bit.
Her eyes slither just enough
to see who might be looking.

Across the street,
in an opposite direction clods a girl,
eleven, perhaps twelve.
A woman's shoes,
carefully selected to match pink slacks out of season;
coiffed with middle-aged hair, she moves to
a languid, lonely tempo as if unsure of the dance.

Lost

Can truest love lose its memory?
Like other living things can it become tethered prey
to time and life and other lurking thieves and just forget?
Can it become distracted and simply lose its way,
falling lost among the thickets, blindly searching for its way home?

Yes, sadly, yes

When its inner light flickers and sputters
like a taper standing just beyond a January door
does it need a sweeping beacon in the long night
or someone to scatter crumbs to guide the way back?

Perhaps, perhaps

But surest of all is an outreached hand.

Take mine and show me the way home.

Short Stories

A Sky Held Captive

Mrs. Fluellen's son died three times during the war. Three separate deaths in three different place, all foreign to him. Three different leavetakings at three different times, each during the night's cold. The first was partially his mother's fault. The second was a shared one. During the final one he felt quite alone. The war, which came to defy his powers of understanding, outlived him by thirty-one hours and fourteen minutes.

His mother did not know of Richard's first death until he wrote her about it a few weeks later. Until then each of his letters had been of great comfort to her. The crooked lines on the small sheets assured her he was still alive and still her son, but somehow a different one. She had never considered Richard to be the cleverest of her children, his sister Jeanette was, but he was her first-born and his letters had begun to tell her something about him. She sensed a deepening of Richard. Something around and through the pages limned another picture of him. Toward the end it began to bother her.

The first letters were full of stories about training camp and the boys he met there. Richard had never been anywhere outside, except across the state line to visit relatives in Illinois. He wrote of the excitement of seeing new places, even if most of it was from a train window. He had even devised a bit of a code in one where he told her about seeing the cow just like the one on Grandpa Beardon's farm. Sometime before returning to camp after his furlough Richard told her the scuttlebutt was that if they were sent to New Jersey they would be shipped to North Africa. Of course, he would not be able to her and Daddy that, but he would try to let them know somehow. Buried in his next letter was a line about seeing that cow. "Don't you see," she explained to Jeanette, "the only cows your grandfather kept were Jerseys. He's telling us his unit's heading to North Africa." There was fighting there, she knew. Gabriel Heatter had talked about it two nights before on the radio.

Richard had written that letter at the end of a very long day. To be on the move finally, maybe heading right into action had filled everyone with nervous energy. Though little shafts of excitement yet burrowed through him, he had calmed down considerably by then. He and Claud Taylor had finally managed to separate themselves from the card games, cigar smoke and fear masquerading as loud voices by making room for themselves in a baggage car. They could not believe their luck at finding quiet. Claud went back to get his ciggies. Richard carried within him a part which did not mind solitude. He had not felt the comfort of being alone since boot camp.

He and Claud and grown up within a block of one another, joined up three weeks apart, and somehow managed to wind up in the same unit heading for the same place. Things were not supposed to work out that way, they knew. It must be admitted they had not really been friends back home. They were a couple of years apart and rarely spent much time around each other, but sharing the distances had brought them together.

Richard did not much dwell on their destination on that trip or, really, on the troop ship later. The officers kept them pretty busy and when he did have time to think it was about home. He knew his family's routine and sometimes, in the safe harbor within his mind, placed himself into it. He knew the hours his mother would be starting meals, when Jeanette and the others would trundle in from school, when his dad would be walking to Smitty's for a quart of Sterling. Most of all he knew when his mother would be worrying about him the most. Those night before she fell asleep.

Most of the real battles had been fought by the time he first drove his ambulance across the hard-packed roads and bedeviling sands. Back home he had worked part-time at Burton's Mortuary. His filed said he only had two years of high school and was listed as semiskilled, chauffer/truck driver. He supposed that was one of the reasons the army had made him an ambulance driver. Perhaps they thought his time in a funeral home made him less chaste about the dead, less likely to turn away from his tasks. If so, the army was mostly wrong.

Back home he had seen a different death. One whose visitations were gentler, or more expected, or accompanied by a soft-treaded serenity. Hell, the worst he had seen was the rye-filled miner who had been trampled by a bank mule. It was no preparation. It did not form a callous hard or thick enough to protect him from what he encountered. Seldom did he sense a feeling of peace anywhere near the men, or parts of men, he placed as gently onto the litters as he could. It was a twisted, frightened, clawing, defiling death he saw. It could be expected, but so random it excited question. They were ugly, squalid, vengeful leavetakings that offered eyes which would not close and faces which would not relax from their rigid, dark-painted masques. He did not understand how any of it could offer up glory to those who remained to march.

He gave those thoughts to Charlie once. Charlie, a buddy assigned to a graves registration detail, was quiet for a long time. "It's the difference between dyin' and gettin' killed," Charlie said finally in his almost painful Arkansas drawl, "the difference between lettin' go and bein' snatched away." Richard told him he was absolutely right. That was how it was. At first he wondered if Charlie had just thought of that during his silence or had been holding it within. Later Richard decided his friend had been carrying it with him a long time.

The truth be told, he did grow slightly more used to it all. By the time he left one continent for another Richard had learned to make his eyes see something other than that at which they looked, made them focus somewhere beyond the scenes which confronted him. Somehow he grew to not register the face, if there was a face, quite so sharply in his mind.

Still, he had discovered as many ways of death as there were men, or children or women, or horses, or... name anything. He came to realize that if you had to die, only to wait for him to find you, and Charlie to bury you, it was better to do so in the Belgian winter than in any of North Africa's seasons. Most of all he found it was better to die and leave behind the wreckage than to simply vanish. It was much less confusing that way.

On a crystal night during the season of a christ when his fogging breath clouded some close-ranging stars Richard holed up with an infantry unit in still another unpronounceable town. He liked those nights when the sky seemed within reach. It was cold, but the stone house in which they gathered blanketed him. If he had the time right his mother was probably peeling potatoes. He had no idea the rumors of his death were about to begin.

A few hours earlier Claud had answered mail call. He received a treasure trove of three letters. Hearing Richard's named called, he convinced a skinny corporal to trust him with his friend's letter. He read his hurriedly, voraciously, before he moved out, placing them in his pocket. He put Richard's letter in his helmet for safekeeping, and so he would not forget. He remembered that his 7th-grade teacher talked about Abe Lincoln doing that back when he clerked in a store.

Around midnight Claud and two new replacements moved through pine trees stiffened with snow to relieve tired men burrowed together at a forward position. Claud knew they were too close together, but had retained a faith in darkness's cloak. Then clear, cold, touchable winter sky thundered like summer.

Richard had heard of it happening, might have even seen it. A shell hitting just right, a mine buried just so, and a man would be gone with its echo. Nothing left. The mortar shell must have been fate-guided, or lucky, or another of the many irrational elements forming a discrete confluence of man, time, and space. Will, the new guy who survived, said there was an explosion and Claud was just no longer there.

That was two days later, after Will woke up. They had found Will and Brevard the next morning. Claud was not there. They found the barrel of his gun, still straight as the day it was made, and his helmet, twisted and charred, with a letter inside.

Richard was not sure how it happened. Probably just the usual confusion after a pull-out under fire. He had to beat it out of the farmhouse when the attack began and it was two days more until he rejoined his unit. Writing to his mother he said he thought it was because her letter to him was the only thing left of the soldier who no longer existed. However it happened, a sergeant in B Company carried around a piece of paper listing Pfc. Richard Fluellen, 18562397, as among the missing, presumed dead, for two days.

Four months later he found himself leaning against what remained of a house's wall in a place called Ettersburg. It was funny he thought because there was a family named Etter back home who owned a grocery store. It was his third straight night there.

Springs, he had come to believe, were cold in Germany. He did not remember them being this cold back home. In his mind he carried with him those April days when a thousand pinpricks of sweat broke out beneath the sweater his mother made him wear, not these chilling days and bone-touching misted nights. He did not think he had really been warm since escaping the thunder covering the farmhouse.

He had awakened again from the silent dream. There was a trace, just the smallest taste, of anger beneath the edge of his tongue, another tiny drop of it rooted in the corner of his eye, just unformed enough to be concealed by the blink of his lid.

In the dream no landscape was to be discerned. No figures, save one, peopled it. It was black; it was grey. Perhaps there was splash of white. It was hard to say. Within it was a paled face crossed by twisted wire, which formed a scar, which etched a history that should not have been lived. The dark eyes looked away. The full mouth would not move. It refused to speak to him. The quiet always shook him awake.

He had heard of the camp before he travelled to it, smelled it before he arrived. He saw it before he realized the toppling stacks of cordwood were not broken trees. What he encountered seemed to be a different species. Humans so degraded that they reversed evolution, becoming throwbacks to a much earlier millennium. Or a new species vaguely humanoid, with parchment skin stretched over a framework of bone. Only a movement of the eyes or hands distinguished the living from the dead.

As they had loaded the truck with medical supplies Major Walker, the surgeon, told them to be careful about giving them food. "Their systems are not used to it," he said softly, edgily. "If you give them too much, or

49

something too rich for them, they might die." What sort of people die if you feed them, Richard recalled thinking.

He should not be out on these streets. They were against orders, these midnight prowls through the tortured nightscapes. He carried no weapon. Three nights before he had encountered the boy, about fourteen, about the same age as his brother Frankie. The boy, blond, slim, wearing some sort of uniform, was climbing the rubble hills, throwing the debris about, whispering "Opa, Opa" over and over again, so quietly, as if he wanted only one to hear him call. His hands and face were blackened by the effort. Silently, without fathomed reason, Richard had bent to aid him with the excavation.

Each night that followed, after the dreaming, after awakening, Richard laced up his boots and return to the digging.

"They no longer hold the sky captive." She had just begun to speak to him as he passed by. It was his second night at the camp. "The stars move once more, rolling release along their tongues, tasting the sweetness of it after a long-parched time."

He was surprised to hear his language coming out of a foreign face the color of day-old ashes. Her hair was short, ragged, patchy, as if some was missing. Her English was quite good, crisp despite the accent. He recognized each word immediately, even if it took them some time for them to acquire a meaning for him. The sentences seemed long practiced, or long thought. He doubted he could express such a thing with his own tongue. He tried to remove the amazement from his voice, saying, stupidly, after an eternity, "You Speak English."

"I have been thinking in it for years now, but this is the first time I have summoned the courage to speak it. My father insisted we learn different languages. One of my brothers learned French, another Italian. He thought it would help us make our way someday. I have listened to you Americans since you arrived four days ago, but only now have I found the will to speak." Her voice was thinned, weak.

Behind her fires burned. They were worried about Typhus and Typhoid, afraid the infections would spread. Richard had spent part of his day with a de-lousing team.

Richard searched for something to say. "What about the stars?"

She seemed embarrassed. "Forgive me, you must. I had feared the world no longer moved. Or they had found some way of chaining the sky above us, of denying us even that. Each night as we marched to the factory and then back again I would look up to the sky, but the stars never seemed to change. It was if they never moved. They seemed so pale, so remote. Not like when I was a child. I would sit with my sister and watch them move over our roof and..." she temporarily struggled for words, "across the city to Grandfather Albert's house."

The fires and the brightening moon bred undulating shadows that crept around them, remarkably softening the eerie, knife-edged harshness of the place, muting the desolation usually etched so deeply by the sunlight. The wraith of a guard tower, occupied now by different uniforms, fell across her face. A few ragged, striped figures combed the shadows incessantly. Most still moved with a strange, ordered, acquired rhythm, never going too near the jagged wire.

"My sister is gone." she said after reading his eyes, "... perhaps they are all gone."

The streets were rather still. Richard was having a hard time getting used to that. The war was moving beyond him. Planes still throbbed above, the occasional quaking boom still shook the horizon. Vehicles of all description and purpose still wound through jumbled streets, but for the most part the cacophony was dwindling. Human sounds began to take precedence again. Each night at about this time he listened for the infant's incessant cry, a wail really, which marched toward him from beyond the church.

She did not give him her name until late on their second night, a night of long silences between them, as each would be. He did not mind the shared quiet. He was, as anyone who knew him would attest, a quiet person. Only at first did it make him uncomfortable. Then he began to appreciate them for what they said to him.

Her name was Devorah, emphasis on the second syllable. Richard had asked her to spell it for him. Kind of like Deborah Heine back home, he told her. For some reason that brought the biggest smile to her. It was then he noticed the missing teeth, and the two broken, jagged ones. Did they fall out or were they hammered away? He wanted desperately to know. But just as desperately he knew there was no answer he could abide to hear just then.

"My name is Devorah Gerstein," she said suddenly across the silence. "Although to them we are all Sarah. Or Israel. I came here from Berlin last year. I have survived."

That flat summation stabbed at him. It came after she talked of labors in a munitions plant each long night. Richard had seen the factory with Gustloff Werke sign on it. In a remote tone she said, "Perhaps my hand made the weapons that killed your comrades. Do you suppose it possible that if I had made one more shell on any of those colliding nights it might have killed you?"

The question caused his mind to stumble. That and hearing his buddies called comrades. It seemed such a foreign word to him. Later she wondered if she were somehow testing him, whether she was looking for a change in his eyes. "No," was all he said. Later he wished he had said something like "I don't think you are capable of that" or "It was not your hand." He was not good at saying such things. But she must have accepted some truth from it. From that point she began to talk more about herself.

One of the klieg lights fastened the heavy dew along the wire, turning it into diamonded beads impaled on the ends of the twisted barbs. It was the girl. Devorah pulled the coarse brown blanket he had brought her up over her shoulders.

Behind her limped the crumpled old man with eyes so submerged he appeared to be a wasted creature looking out at you from deep within a cave. In his shuffle the left foot always carefully stepped in the light, the right always found a shadow. Bare patches of gray-white hair clung to the head and face which seemed entirely comprised of bone. His arms were much, much too long for what remained of his body. The old man roamed the camp ceaselessly. Richard ran into him everywhere. Sometimes, he would seize Richard's foreign arm and mutter something indecipherable. Each time he would look straight at Richard and slowly swivel his head at the lack of understanding.

Richard pointed to him. "Who is that old man? What is that he is always saying?"

Devorah did not have to turn to know who it was.

"That is Aron. We call him Aron the cantor. He was a Hazan somewhere in the east. He wants to talk of nothing but the Hester Panim... the hiding away of God's face. He angers many, many people with it. They do not want to hear of it."

"I...," sometimes he felt impotent in front of her knowledge, her life, "I don't understand."

The Torah says that God might turn away from his people at some point." Richard was pretty sure that was the Jew's bible, and he tried to nod with some assurance.

Devorah closed her eyes and leaned forward in an act of remembrance.

"Then my anger will flare against them in that day and I will abandon them and hide my face from them, and they shall be devoured by many evils."

She opened her eyes once again and turned them to his. "There are those who believe we have angered God so terribly that he has turned away from us, so this terrible evil visited upon us is a retribution.

53

He had only been there a few days, but the first ten seconds had been enough. He looked around. "What could have been so terrible to deserve this?"

She rocked forth slowly; he wanted to reach out and catch her. "Aron says it could be anything.... from breaking dietary laws to... simply losing faith. Perhaps such things are not soon known. Or never to be understood."

Richard Fluellen, son of a woman who was faith, shook his head. This was not his mother's God. Or Father Harney's God. The slim priest back home had told his class of original sin, and a father's sins, and mortal sins, but Richard remembered no threats of punishment on earth like this, or intended for all.

He felt the stupidity rise within him, "But... why... everyone... why...?"

Without realizing it, he was sure, she made for him a face that said he would never understand. It made him feel small, and undergrown and so distant from her world, and fearful that she thought him incapable of crossing a chasm separating her from all. There was the longest pause between the movement of her lips and the sound that worked its way from them, "I do not know. Perhaps all are to be part of one."

"Do you think this," he searched once more through the things he had seen, "was a turning away?"

"Who can know, least of all me. Possibly it ... is the only answer that allows faith to live."

Without knowing why, knowing he shouldn't, he could not leave it alone. This must be hurting her greatly, he remembered thinking. He looked away.

"But why... who could be so bad... I know women, children, ... Christ, children ... children were..." He could not think of it any longer.

Devorah left him to the silence.

Richard made himself breathe.

Before he knew it, asshole he thought of himself at the same time, the words escaped his trembling, well-fed, unbroken body, "What could you have possibly...." I mean I can't imagine you...."

She made a distance from him. She did not look angry, or hurt, just quite, quite alone. Devorah's always fidgeting body suddenly became becalmed, as if she had been waiting for very long time to answer such a question and only wanted her voice to speak for her. She looked someplace he could not see.

"I do not know."

They barely spoke for the rest of that night, just sat there beneath a bright, squandered moon. At intervals she would seem ready to speak, but something always took away her will, always drug he back to where she was.

He watched over her. Her body became a compressed version of itself, her thinned legs pulled to her chest, her weak arms holding her together. She could not find a stillness. Sometimes, her shoulders and head would tremble with an unseemly violence, as if fighting off a sudden, deep chill. He ached to reach for her. For a moment or two, never long, her body would find a pool of repose and relax its journey, but never for long. Her lower lip would jerk, or her left hand would shake as it reached out or pulled back to form a shield. The shaking would start all over again.

Try as he might, as much as he wished it, Richard had no words within him to balm such a ravagement. But, did anyone? He doubted any of the poets or thinkers he had ignored in the books in Sister Mary Thomas' class could do any more. He just watched over her, trying his damnedest never to turn his eyes away from her. He did not want her to think him capable of turning away. He just watched her and hovered close in case she wished to touch him, or showed any sign that he was to touch her. The reliving, he thought, must have been worse than the living of it. It must overshadow all that came before.

Finally, when she said she must sleep, he touched her shoulder, so softly he was unsure if he had done it. It was the first time. She traced the back of his hand with one hand before rising to walk away.

These nights, these damned nights, villains of nights. He should not be here. The baby's cry faded. He walked on. Ahead a dark figure arose from a shadow. It startled him somehow to see someone dressed as he, wearing his uniform.

"You.. we... should not be out here, son. You know that." His hands were filled with fidgeting, burnished beads.

Once, Richard would have been filled with schoolboy guilt. "I know, Father, couldn't sleep."

"I know we've eased up a bit on curfew, but if you get caught...."

"Yeah, you're right. I'll be careful. I won't be out long. Just needed to stretch my legs."

"Well, don't make it a hike. Everything okay, son?"

"Fine, Father," in a tone that Buck, captain of all the teams back at St. Leonard's, had used when Father Harney had asked how practices had gone.

"Well, be on with you then. Say, you've been writin' to the folks back home, haven't you?" It was his standard line. Crossley, the company's resident wiseass, always said that Father Yates was more concerned with morale at home than the troops'.

He hadn't written home in two weeks. Now he wanted to write his mother the longest letter ever. Not the usual stuff, he thought, but these letters that seemed like he was talking to her. Letters that he thought were full of serious things. Telling her about the girl he met and what they talked about. Serious stuff that professors or someone would talk about. He started composing it in his mind as he entered the camp.

"I have been waiting for you. I worried you might not wish to return" She was smiling. He had been worried she might not want to see him. She seemed genuinely happy to see him. He immediately fell into her dark, brown eyes.

They just fell into talking. Maybe he did most of the listening.

She talked about some of the other soldiers. "You Americans just don't look like soldiers. I like that. You look more like workers waiting to go home. Though, many of you do not look at us."

For a while she talked about Berlin and wondered if it was still there. "My father said they did not hate us so until after the last war. He threw away his medal from that war after they took our garments for the Winterhilfe."

When he offered her some chocolate she said she had never been a child for sweets. She liked breads and fruits. How her grandmother could bake bread that was better than any cake. Her favorite treat was the pineapple her father would surprise her with on special occasions.

Once, from out of nowhere, she said, "I so wish to shampoo my hair, with real soap, and then to let grow long as before. You would not credit it, but it was once quite lovely. It was my best feature. The only thing in the mirror that gave me pleasure."

Richard hesitated, but plunged in. "I can too certainly believe that." Should he say it? Did he have the right? "I think you are pretty."

She smiled as if being told a lovely fairy tale, something to conjure with, but not believe for a second. "Such kindness you have. But you must not feel you have to say such things. Vanity does not last long in a place like this. I was never the pretty one. My sister, ... oh, she was lovely."

He wanted to shake her until she believed.

"No, I can't even make myself beautiful in my imagination." She said it with such total self-faith, so matter-of-factly, that he felt sadder than he could ever recall.

Devorah seemed not to notice. "I have talked so much. I wish to listen to your voice. Tell me of America. Talk to me of Indiana and your home there. I always thought Indiana sounded like the most American place. A whole state named after red Indians. My brother loved to read the Karl May stories about the wild west and cowboys and Indians."

Richard had lived in Indiana his whole life and never really thought about how it got its name. She had a way of thinking, of talking, that moved him. He spent an hour or more telling her about his mother and dad, about the little sisters and brothers always tugging at him. How mean he sometimes thought his oldest sister had been. How she had put his cat under his rowboat and said nothing as he looked for it for that whole week. He talked and talked, and it felt good.

When she was spent from the memories, she stood and looked around the camp. "See here the slaves."

He started to speak again.

"You must not," she faltered, "for so long there has been no pity here but our own. Now, I see it everywhere. I see it in your eyes, and it makes me sad. People can only live with the pity of others for so long."

She settled back alongside him as if satisfied with her search. "Do you know what you... the... victors... what will be done with us when the war is over?

He held no answer for her.

"I am glad you told me of your family." It made him feel good, warm. He left that night with some hope growing within him.

Richard made his way to the building. For the second night in a row the boy had not appeared. He climbed up a small hill of rubble and bent over, removing bricks, frosted still with the mortar meant to hold them together, and tossed them down the side of the pile. They joined the darkened brands of wood, the lengths of steel, twisted, but yet strong, fashioned by another generation of Kruppianer, and the arm in a grey sleeve from a day or two before. He just kept digging.

After a half hour he climbed down from the pile. He sat down, leaned against the wall, and reached for his Camels.

That last night he had hurried to the camp. In a cloth bag he carried two pineapples he had liberated from a mess truck. Crossley had a buddy who was an aide to some high-living colonel in G-2 who might be able to swipe some real shampoo in exchange for some trophy like a Nazi flag or a Luger.

He looked all over the camp, until he ran into the fat sargeant from graves registration. "It don't make a fucking bit of sense," he offered. "Why would anyone who lived through this walking hell turn around and give away their life again? I found her in a pool of blood with a strand of barbwire wrapped around her wrists and throat." Suddenly all was gone. The people were gone, blockhouses invisible, all around was a void. "They found her right after the General forced the townspeople to come and see what this hellhole was."

Mother of Christ, he thought, this is the coldest place on earth. He walked past the church, or what remained of it. He looked up to see the twisted rope hanging from a tower. Sometimes he imagined it as being severed from the bell, sometimes he thought it the remnant of a noose.

In a confluence of time, places, and events, and more than a small world away, Richard Fluellen's mother put her youngest son in a galvanized washtub when whatever force holding together a brick wall in a cratered German town relaxed its grip.

A Light Beyond These Woods

A May day on a visit to his hometown. Jonathan had called her from his brother's house around ten. He had awakened her. Which surprised him. He still knew the Mary Margaret of years past, who usually awoke early to greet the day with expectations. Ever the waterman's daughter she rose early. Groggily she had said something about her sister (the one he liked, not the sour one) maybe visiting and something she had done the night before. She needed her sleep, she said. Could she call him back later? "Sure," he said. "give me call when you are ready." He owed her that

His brother and his family had gone to church (still an alien concept to him) and he tried to nap on the couch he shared with his niece Amanda's cat (he hated cats), but it was not to be. He could never entertain sleep when he most wanted it. Instead he replayed his father-in-law's news, relayed eighteen months before through Mary Margaret's colleague, that the woman who was once so much part of his life had lung cancer. It had not made sense. She had never smoked. Maybe she had been right that her office at the college was a prime example of sick building syndrome.

His tentative, throat tightening phone call her to her had been their first communication in five years, except for an email sent to her three days earlier. "Hello," it had said, "you may not want to hear from me, but I will be in town this weekend and I would like to see you." She had responded by saying she thought it was time they talked and included her new phone number.

At a loss about what to do with himself until she called, he showered and went to roam the aisles of a used-book store. Amid the mysteries, his niece called to ask if he would be at her house when she got home. She really wanted to see him before he left. How do you explain to a seven-year old who adores her uncle that he has to face his past instead of playing games with her? "I'm sorry, baby, but I have a long drive home. I'll be back in a few weeks for your birthday and we'll have fun then. I love you." Somehow it did not seem enough.

Finally the call. "I'm sorry," she said, "it is just that the treatments wear me out so much I sometimes have to sleep twelve hours a day. You can come over now if you still want to"

"I understand." Jonathan said, though he was not sure he did. "I'll be there in ten minutes."

The drive was an eon and an instant. Up a street he knew so well. A street he and his wife, Anne, had lived on when first married. Past the drug store, beyond a Dairy Queen, across the seemingly interminable number of railroad tracks in his decrepit hometown. Past the student ghetto of sad houses that once held families, but now had been split into shabby apartments for college students forced to live on the cheap. The town had always depressed him, but ten years removed from it and the damn place could sometimes edge him into despondence. "Fucking town," he whispered to himself, "I don't need this today."

He knew where her new house was. Each time he or he and his wife had driven by his eye had looked toward it and wondered if she was in there. Wondered what might happen if she were standing on her porch as they passed and their eyes met. He pulled into a side street and took a deep breath as he turned off the car. Sat there just a while, gathering strength or courage or just postponing the meeting for a few seconds more.

He forced his feet down the sidewalk and up the steps to her door. In the time between the bell's ping and Mary-Margaret's opening of the door Jonathan replayed their years as friends. They both comforted him and issued a stinging slap across his face.

She pulled open the door slowly, as if she too wanted to hold back the inevitable. Had she too imagined what this moment would be like? Like Jonathan, had she surmised that it might be a chance encounter at the mall, walking into a restaurant to see a familiar face at a corner table, or a glance into the next lane into a car stopped at a light? He certainly had. At times during his trips home, in places he knew she might be, he had felt a prickling on his neck. Each time he silently urged Anne to make her purchase or lose interest so they might be safely on their way. Had she thought the same thoughts? He knew she had.

Finally, the time could be stilled no longer. The door swung open. She was there. He tried to make his face a mask.

Though he had tried a thousand times to picture what she would be like, this was not it. She was heavier. No, that was not right. She seemed bloated, puffy. Suddenly his old joke after seeing Nanci Griffith perform, that something must be wrong with her, that she was "puffy, late Elvis Nanci," seemed incredibly cruel.

Next he saw the wig. It was near the color of her real hair, but not quite, and curlier. God, her hair. She was the first person he had ever heard use the term "bad hair day." It became their running joke. Each morning she would struggle with her fine hair. Whether she succeeded in corralling it or not was the portent of her day to come. Often the first thing she said was when he called or saw her was, "I am having a bad hair day," or, "I am having a good hair day and life is worth living."

It had always made him laugh. It was Mary Margaret.

Now, he knew, a bad hair day was watching curls fall languidly onto sterile floors. "Come on in then," she said. Her voice weaker, not quite the pitch he recalled. They both just stood in her entryway. Neither quite looking directly at the other. Beyond her ashed face, over her shoulder, stood an absurd Chinese figurine. Not at all her taste he thought. Too kitschy. Must have been a gift from someone whose feelings she must shelter.

"You look good. More gray in your beard than I remember, but it has been five years. I like. It brings out your eyes." She had always liked his blue eyes.

What to say? There was no compliment that would not ring false in both their ears. "It's good to see you. Thanks for letting me come by."

"Why of course. I have never denied you." Was that a simple statement of fact, or a gently offered dagger, Jonathan wondered? Was she casting him as an apostate apostle?

"Still, I am glad you said yes. I just wanted to see you."

She just gave him a sideways smile. Thirty seconds more of silence.

"I have Diet Coke and chocolate on offer," she said. Their long evenings together usually involved diet soda and chocolate at some time. Later, they shifted to glasses of cheap wine for her and rum for him. "Come into the kitchen and help me."

The kitchen was at the back of the house, with windows on three sides. The afternoon sun touched every corner. "Can you get the glasses? They're on the top shelf there." Though she was tall for a woman, about 5'10", she always had him get things off the top shelf for her.

"I like the kitchen. Very airy."

"Yes it's quite a change from that small kitchen in my apartment. Remember how dark it could be? At least it had that window over the sink, remember?"

He did. Recalled that when a new man had moved in next door his kitchen window looked out on hers, she had turned their occasional waves at each other into a fantasy romance that never became reality.
Drinks poured, she said, "Let's go into the living room."

In one corner was the wooden bookcase he had helped her haul up the steep stairs in her old apartment on a sweltering July day shortly after her divorce. Due to a superstition he always suspected she made up on the spot, she insisted that it could not be moved empty, that one book had to remain on the shelves. One step from the landing the book had finally slipped. In a perfectly described arc it slammed into his crotch. He managed to push the bookcase onto the landing before doubling over. He looked down to see it was volume of what Anne would call a "lusty busty bodice ripper."

He had just started laughing. "Jesus, Mary Margaret, you damn near castrate me with that crap! If I am going to lose use of my penis, couldn't it have been Joyce?" They had sat on the landing for five minutes, laughing, sweat erupting, discussing what authors (Updike, Le Carre, Wodehouse) Jonathan might find worth forfeiting his manhood to.

The bookcase was once again filled. Besides books there were two shelves of videotapes. All carefully labeled, he knew. Mary Margaret was an inveterate taper. The Today Show, her soap, music performances. One of her rituals was the marking of her TV Guide. Each week, she would devour it for programs she wanted to see, but could not be home when they aired. A friend had dubbed her a popular culture maven.

The same tan couch that he remembered. But two or three chairs were new to him, including a blue recliner. Recliners were never her style. She pointed to it. "Sit there. The salesman said it is perfect for tall men. I told him I had a friend who was 6"10" and he said you would love it. I'm glad you are finally getting to try it."

"It is great. I like this room," Jonathan said. "It is very comfortable."

"I love it. It's one of the reasons I bought the house. I love that it is sort of oblong. The house was built in 1946. I love the fireplace. Do you think it is the original fireplace? You are the historian, after all."

"Hell, you were always better at architecture and styles than I. I am a social historian, remember? But I would say the mantle is 1960s, but that is just a guess."

"Yes. I remember when you spoke to my women's history class and one of the students asked you to define what being an historian meant and you said that you were a 'just a professional rememberer.'" God, I was proud of you for that. I think you made that poor freshman all dewy-eyed and wet." He smiled. He remembered that day, too. He was proud that she was so proud to have him there.

"How is Anne?"

"She's fine. She's presenting at a conference in Denver this weekend. So, I decided to come home to visit the family. I don't get back much these days. She is Associate Dean now."

"Yes, congratulate her for me. I ran into her dad at a brunch. He told me. He is certainly proud of her. Tell her I asked about her."

Something in the way she said that made Jonathan file it away in his mind.

"And your grandmother?" Jonathan's grandmother had liked Mary Margaret. Always asked about her, though she often confused her name with a local Catholic church and called her Margaret Mary.

"She is great. She'll be 102 next month. Outside of her hearing and occasional memory lapses you would guess she was thirty years younger. You know my grandma. She is the strongest person I have ever known. She's living with my uncle now." When asked, he had always told granny Mary Margaret was fine. He did not want her to know they no longer saw one another.

They sat pretending to be engrossed in drinking their soda. Mary Margaret just smiled through the silence. Jonathan pretended to inspect the room. Finally she said, "You look thinner to me."

"I suppose I am a bit. I took up bike riding with a vengeance a few years ago. Splurged on a first class bike. Last summer I was riding about 125 miles a week."

"It shows. In one of the documentaries I thought your face looked heavier. You were quite the talking head for a while. I have several of them on tape. I take them out and watch them every once in a while. You are really quite good at it."

"Oh, it allows me a chance to pontificate on occasion. Actually, one of the producers I work with said I was good at talking in sound bites. I told him I did not consider that a compliment"

"Still, you come across well. I always got excited when I saw you appear on the screen. I was proud. Nikki was here once when you came on and she threw a pillow at the TV and called you a shallow heartless bastard. But you two never got along."

Jonathan smiled, "No, not much."

"But when the Lincoln documentary was on my friend, Grace, you don't know her, was here and she said 'So that is the famous asshole Jonathan that Nikki loathes? Impressive, it would be interesting to meet him.' We spent the rest of the evening drinking wine and discussing you."

Jonathan was sure they had. Equally sure that whatever conclusion was drawn was best not discussed at this point.

They talked at each other for 15 stilted minutes. He asking her about her family and work, she about his work.

She got up abruptly. He noticed she supported herself by leaning against the chair. He asked if she needed to sit down.

"No... no, I would love to show you my house."

She took him through the downstairs, pointing out things she liked about each room. In the dining room was the big walnut table where she served him steak dinners and huge breakfasts when he visited. A small sitting room decorated with so many things he remembered. The delicate fan from a grateful Asian student she had tutored. The picture of her father on his boat (she always said Jonathan reminded her of him). The LBJ campaign button he and Anne had bought her in an antique store on one of her visits to their house. Surprisingly, a picture of him and Mary Margaret, Jonathan sitting on her desk with a book in his hand and Mary Margaret beaming a broad smile, taken in her office at the college.

His eye must have lingered on it, because she said, "I did not put that out because you were coming. It was in a drawer until about six weeks ago. But something made me take it out again. Come, let me show you the upstairs."

At the top of the stairs they entered a room that occupied the entire length of the house. "Here it is, the Benton Music Palace."

The Benton Music Palace. Somehow that irritated him terribly. After Jonathan had removed himself from her life Mary Margaret had begun hosting house concerts. She would bring in musicians, usually folkies, and invite friends and the public to hear them play. He guessed she charged a small admission and the hat was passed and if they had CDs the artists would sell them to people who became instant fans who felt they had shared an intimate experience with a real performer. Christ.
When he had first heard about it a deep anger rose within Jonathan. Why had something that was so Mary Margaret, ever the adoring fan of any musician she liked, doing something he knew made her incredibly happy, made him so crazy? He was not sure, but it did. He had first heard about it through an article in a local paper Anne's father had sent them. Later, he had searched for her on the net and her website, read her accounts of the concerts.

What turns, spasms, convolutes inside you that makes things you once adored about someone turn rancid, Jonathan wondered? Is it you or them? You probably. You certainly. They are just being themselves, but you see it differently. Is it pain or heartbreak, or anger or a perverted, ugly, soul-wasting, heart-immolating, self-eviscerating sense of self-preservation? At this point, he had not a single fucking clue. Not a single fucking, goddamn, sonuvabitching clue. He wondered if he ever would.

She loved music. Like him she had no talent in that arena, but she loved it. Also like him, she knew music could speak to the most hidden, sacred parts of her. A song, a few notes could take her to a place. He saw it on her face sometimes. Certain songs transported her to the past, erased the time/space continuum. That past, that place became reality. Not the gray, monochrome existence she was forced to live in by day, but the rich, multi-hued life of the mind and soul. Once more like him, she knew that was the place she preferred to live, had to inhabit, to feel alive. Fuck reality, go to hell convention, shove it up your ass you church-going, Rotary-breakfasters, I make my own place, choose my world. In that they were soul mates.

Her tastes were much broader than his. Including country music. Which she tried to make him listen to. She would gush about Lyle or Trisha or some other yahoo and make him a tape of songs meant to convey a message from her to him. Once, he had been receptive to them. ("Jesus Christ, Mary Margaret, show some discernment. It is not all good," he had hissed in one of his last conversations with her. "You can't love everybody and everything.").

"This was the teenaged son's room. When the realtor showed it to me I knew it would be the perfect setting for my concerts. I really love this house, Jonathan. It has truly become home. The only thing missing is the lanai."

The lanai. That is what they called the porch in her second storey apartment. The lanai could seem a magic place. Decorated with flowers and plants it had been the setting for some of his happiest moments. With music wafting out the door from her stereo, they would sit for endless hours. It had been the forging place of their true friendship. The place where they sat for hours, discussing their lives, music, dreams, hurts, the realities that intervened in and stole pieces of their souls. Where they discussed the mundane, and, to them, the sacred. Where they ridiculed the foolish, again to them, and exalted in the thoughts that separated them from others.

The lanai. Where, on soft nights that usurped the cares of the everyday, they sipped rum or wine, felt time suspended, and the world excluded. Where he talked to her about things and picked at old scabs. Told her more things about himself than he did anyone, but Anne. And she did the same. Each knowing they could.

"I miss the lanai," he said.

For the first time on this visit he felt she looked at him with the face of his old friend, "I do too. More than you know."

She took his hand, "Well, I feel the need for chocolate. Let's go downstairs and raid the candy bowl."

Mary Margaret sat the bowl on the floor between them. He pulled out three packages of peanut M&Ms, she a Hershey bar. As he popped four candies into his mouth, knowing he could wait no longer, he said, "So, tell me about the cancer."

She drew a long breath and leaned her head back. "You remember my incessant cough... do you realize how many times we have spoken the word remember today?"

He did.

"Well, it just got worse. I never felt quite right. What can I say... it got worse. I couldn't walk up the stairs without feeling weak. They did tests, X-rays. On a July day... it was such a lovely day... I remember on the drive to doctor's office how beautiful the clouds were... for some reason, I think because her office was near the street where you and Anne had that cute house, I realized your birthday was coming up. I wondered if I should send you a card. I suppose I thought it might open some floodgate in you and you would call. You know how romantic I can be? Anyway, that was the day I found out."

"It was funny. You wonder how you will react when someone tells you are going to die. Does that sound dramatic? Well, it was so strange. I took it very calmly. Oh, I later went through all the stages they talk about, denial, anger, all that, but that day I was calm. That is not like me. You know that.

On the drive home I thought about how I was going to tell my mother and my sisters. How I was going to tell my friends. What words I would use. You know me. I played out the conversations in my head. Trying to get them right. It pleased me to know that, at least then, my first thought was about them, how to make it easier on them.'

"That doesn't surprise me," Jonathan said.

"Well, this might. When I got home, after just sitting here drinking wine for an hour or so, I picked up the phone and started dialing… I had dialed six or seven numbers when I realized it was yours I was calling. I put the phone down."

She told him the details of her treatment, the doctors, the nurses who were so kind. Christ, Jesus Fucking Christ, fuck, fuck, fuck, something inside Jonathan shriveled. Who knew that when they ended almost five years of silence brutish words like metastasize chemo, and stage four would be part of it?

"How long," he asked, fearing the answer.

"Maybe a month, two. Hard to say."

Jonathan just looked at her.

"I am leaving for Virginia next week. Mom and Elaine and Joanie want me to die at home. I do, too."

Jonathan never felt like a less capable human being. "I am sorry."

"Do you remember, that word again, when you said that all life was subtext? That the obvious, what we subconsciously agreed upon as reality, what we call everyday life, was unimportant? That what really mattered was lurked below the surface?

"Yes," Jonathan said. It was one of his pet theories about life.

"This is one of those times, isn't it?"

"Yes."

She gave him a sad smile.

"Do you still listen to Nanci," she asked?

She always felt she had "discovered" Nanci Griffith. Mary Margaret had lived in Austin for a time when her ex-husband had struggled—and eventually failed—to get tenure. She had loved Austin. In some small club there she first saw Nanci Griffith and fell in love with her songs, most particularly "There's a Light Beyond These Woods (Mary Margaret). In her sweet way, she always felt the song was written to her. She was a Johnny Appleseed for Nanci (she always referred to her favorites by their first name, as if they were her dear friends, which, of course, they were in a way), spreading her music to any new acquaintance who showed any interest. She had every album she ever recorded. One of Mary Margaret's prized tapes was a live performance and interview Nanci had given on an Austin radio station she had recorded while her diffident husband watched the Super Bowl. It was one of the first gifts she had given Jonathan.

"Yes, of course…some of her stuff."

Her look told him she was afraid to ask if he listened to "There's a Light…." He was glad. He had not been able to play that song in years.

"Who else do you listen too now?"

"Oh, Gorka, Lighfoot, Shindell. Joni, of course. Joni has written my life for twenty year now. Often she was a few years ahead of me, but I always caught up with her, for good or ill. I really haven't added many new people. I listen to mostly classical music now."

She smiled. "I remember that conference trip to Chicago with Jake. You excused yourself from the reception and I found you later in your room, alone, feet up, smoking a cigar and listening to Kindertotenlieder. You looked so sad. I will never forget that."

"I wasn't sad, just contemplative."

"No, you were sad, deeply sad. Why will you never admit that? I saw you. I know you. Something in that night took you to a dark place. There was a chasm between you and your eyes. It scared me. Made me feel alien. Made me feel not a part of you. I hoped I would never see it again, but, of course, I did (Another dagger, Jonathan wondered?). I saw it that last afternoon you were with me."

"Jake said later you were putting on a show for me. He said you were always playing the dark, melancholy Irish poet, because some women like that. But he never saw you quite right. Any more than you did him."

Ah… Jake, a colleague with whom Jonathan had always had a complicated relationship. It seemed they were always dancing a skittish, dissembling pas de deux. They always pretended to like each other, but a sensed aura of rivalry and ineluctable testing of one another made that a mutually understood illusion.

Oh, Christ, Jake, he thought. Fucking Jake Bondurant. Dead seven years and his ghost still haunted.

Mary Margaret's long, damaging, unrequited passion for the married Jake (which Jonathan always thought Jake subtly encouraged) had been a running theme of their friendship. For hour upon seemingly endless hour he had listened to her analyze her relationship with Jake. Listened as she parsed every conversation, each encounter, every sidelong look, played the oracle divining the message of every tossed bone. (An apt metaphor, he had told her with a cold venom in his voice during one of their last conversations, Jake was always tossing you a bone. Even on the phone he could feel how that rapier thrust had devastated her. Sometimes, Jonathan thought as he said it, I can be a complete bastard.)

72

Jonathan had literally held her hand at breakfast on an earlier trip with Jake while she, in a quiet, searing bout of self humiliation, recounted how she had offered herself to Jake in the hotel room next to Jonathan's the night before, but had been refused. He had been suborned by her desperation to know how Jake was and agreed to call Jake's wife at the hospital at midnight as he lay dying. He had visited Jake at the hospital at her request, painfully talking to him from behind a glass panel. Even then the dance continued, but he had done it for her.

Jake, she had once told him, was convinced Jonathan and Mary Margaret were having an affair. His evidence for that flight of fancy, or assuaging of guilt, was the way Jonathan had touched her shoulder one afternoon when Jake had visited.

She suddenly looked lost, inhabiting somewhere he could not go. Somewhere beyond. For a second he thought she was dying there in front of him. He leaned forward toward her. As if sensing him again, she looked right at him.

"What happened to us?" she asked in a whisper. "What happened to us?"

The question he came for. The question he dreaded. The question he could not begin to answer.

Oh, sweet Christ, Jonathan thought. What to say? Do I tell you that I was afraid that you, you who asked so many questions of me over the years, would ask me a question I did not want to answer? That, deep in your soul, you did not wish confirmation. A question I was afraid to answer as much as much as you feared the reply? Why, why, why, why, Jesus fucking Christ, why would you even think of seeking the answer? Did you fear my response? Didn't you know the answer? Didn't you know that any other answer than the one I would give would meant abandoning my soul, my sense of me? Sometimes, if you truly love someone, you swallow the pain and self-doubt and selfishness and consign yourself to a sort of self-martyrdom?

"It was me," Jonathan said. "My fault, not yours. It was something in me. Don't blame yourself. It was me, not you."

Mary Margaret just looked at him.

She grew quiet again. Then she leaned forward and took his hand. Fixed her eyes on his. "Jonathan, Jonathan, my sweet man," she said, "please just listen. I have waited for five years to say these things. I know you came here for many reasons. One of them was guilt. You feel you abandoned me. And you did. You did, for whatever reason, you did. I do not comprehend it all, but I accept it now."

He must have left his face unguarded for a split second, because she paused, only to begin in an impatient tone, "No, no, just listen, please just listen. I only have so much strength left."

"Understand this. I had known you, what, two years when Richard divorced me? You and I were friends. But just that. But then you became more than just someone I knew. Do you know how I felt then? Richard had only made love to me once in a year. On Valentine's Day. Out of a sense of obligation, I suspect. He had already started his affair with Colleen. When he left me I went home and cried every night, every god damned night. I felt like a failure. I felt like shit."

"Then you truly came into my life. You made me laugh. God, you made me laugh. Do you know you made me laugh again? You knew when to listen. You knew when to talk. You knew when say something awful about Richard, when to say something sweet about me. You probably do not remember this, but once when I was wearing shorts you quite offhandedly said "Nice legs, Mary Margaret.' That carried me for weeks."

He did remember saying that and had meant it.

"Do you know what that means? You cared for me. You gave me hope. You made me feel deserving. You made me feel good about myself. You loved me."

Mary Margaret leaned forward. "Yes, I fell in love with you. I know that scared you. But I did. Accept it. You deserved it. Remember that time we went shopping at the mall for the perfect purse? The saleslady told me I was lucky to have a husband who would shop with me. I did not tell her you were just my friend. I wanted her to think I could have a husband like you. I know that made you feel uneasy, but it made me feel so good, so valued. You did that for me. You made me feel good about myself. There was a time when I did not think that was possible."

"I was 45, was never a beauty queen. I had to find a fulltime job and live on my own for the first time ever. I was so scared, so scared. I had Jill and Mary, and Nikki to lean on, and they were such good friends, but… it was you …"

He could think of nothing to say.

"Yes, you broke my heart when you just left my life. Just walked away and pretended I did not exist. My heart broke a bit every day I did not hear from you. It was cruel. I saw it coming. Knew what you were doing. You had never said anything hurtful to me ever before. But when you turned that sardonic wit of yours on me and my life, I knew. I used to revel in that wit when you directed it at people I didn't like. So I knew how you could dissect someone. When you said some of those things, I knew, I just knew. I know how stubborn you can be. That once you began a journey, you would not turn back knew if you walked away, you would never come back. I could not stop it. Did Anne ever tell you I even contacted her to see what I could do to at least make you talk to me again?"

He wanted to look away from her, but couldn't. Some medicine must be choked down. "No."

"But… but, you gave me something so vital before that. It sustained me. It allowed me to get over the hurt. It made me stronger. I learned. In the end I did that on my own. You helped. What you had given me gave me strength, but I did it. I did it. I did it on my own. I won't say I thought about you every day over the last few years, but it was close. I went on with my life. I enjoyed my life. My life would have been even better with you in it. I like to think yours would have been better with me in yours"

Mary Margaret just stopped there. She leaned back and closed her eyes.

"Yes," he said so softly he wondered if she heard him, "it would have been."

Mary Margaret said nothing. Just sat there, eyes closed, breathing softly.

"Well, I am tiring you out. And I still have a long drive ahead of me. I should be going."

"Yes, I understand. And I am very tired." She rose slowly from the chair. He wondered if he should help her to her feet, but her eyes said no.

"Thank you for coming." She hesitated. Started to speak, stopped, then said, "It... I... I am glad you called. I wanted to see you... hear your voice. See your eyes one more time. Thank you. It was important to me. It is just... I know you distrust what you called Phil Donahue talk, but... I... we... needed some sort of closure... some tieing of loose ends It is something I do a lot these days. It is a comfort, really it is. Try to understand that. You might think I am crazy, but sometimes I think I have been given a great gift. I know how and when I am going to die. It allows for reckonings and homecomings. Believe me, I am glad you came."

Jonathan knew she was right. That is why he had come, too. He just looked into her eyes, then closed his own for a second. Deep within he felt something wrinkle, something convulse, something like a stillborn sob echo through him.

"I am glad I did, too."

They walked into the entryway. Just stood there for a while.

In a flash he thought, she has taught me how to face death with grace. Could I do the same? He doubted it.

She looked at him with expectant eyes. He bent down. Wrapped his long arms around her. A last embrace before a dying they both knew was coming soon. Felt the strength in a wasting body. He put his head on her shoulder. Felt her false hair shift against his ear as his tear slid down onto her shoulder. "I won't come to your funeral," he said, "don't ask that of me."

She pulled back. Took his face in her hand and pulled it lower. They were face to face. He could feel her breath wash across his lips. "I would never ask that of you. You came today, because you wanted to. Because I wanted you to. You knew that. That is enough. Today was our mourning. Today was our day..... today was us."

Her breath came in heaves as she spoke.

His seemed to cease.

"I love you," he said.

"I know."

He could say no more. Just looked at her and kissed her on the cheek. He turned for the door. Her hand reached out and gently touched him on the back. He felt a tear fall and etch a path down her pale cheek.

He walked down her steps.

He did not look back.

That would come later

Epilogue: Word of her death came 17 days later, heralded by a mournful ping. Jonathan was one more cc: on a list of thirty, saying everyone's best friend was gone. Is my conceit any less than twenty-nine others, he thought, in believing that she would have saved that particular designation only for me? Perhaps not, perhaps so.

An Unquiet Mind and a Feckless Soul

I suppose I should start out by telling you how I came to know the story pf Moses "Mozzie" Harper. My granddad's brother, Forrest, died in Arizona in 1979. I had never met him. He had no family. Gramps asked me to drive out to Arizona to arrange to have his body back home and collect his stuff. Forrest had been in law enforcement all his adult life: Sheriff's Deputy, MP in the Army, a Pinkerton and ended up as prison guard in Arizona.

He knew he was dying so he had arranged some things. As he wished I gave his furniture and clothes to a charity. I headed back to Indiana with two lock boxes and an old Army footlocker. The lock boxes had the names of Gramps and his sister Alma. Turned out there were family photos and cash in each for both of them. There was no name on the footlocker.

I suppose it was about six weeks after the funeral that Gramps asked me lug up the footlocker from the basement. When we opened it we found his Army uniform, several MP arm bands, a couple of his badges and three pistols. There was an old manila envelope, but it looked like it just had old newspaper clippings so we set it aside. Gramps decided to keep the uniform and a pistol. The other two guns he gave to me and my brother saying we should keep them in remembrance of a man we never knew.

About a month later I was visiting Gramps and remembered the envelope. While Gramps was taking a nap I took the envelope out to his sun porch and opened it. Every clipping was about Moses Harper. Accounts of his crimes and trial and his time in the state Prison in where Forrest was a guard. Down at the bottom of the pile was a 16 page manuscript in a neat refined hand. It was Moses' life story written at the request of a prison psychologist.

In between some of the pages were little annotations written by Forrest. The first note described Moses as a very smart man who scored very high on IQ tests but did evil things. Forrest became friendly with him. He said Moses had a clever sense of humor and was well read. As I read and re-read the manuscript I found that the tone varied, partially I suppose, because it was written over the course of 8 to 10 days. In some passages his intelligence is evident and he tells a coherent story showing a dry sort of humor. Some parts, mainly dealing with descriptions of his crime are almost streams of consciousness with little punctuation or coherent sentence structure. A note from Forrest explained that there were days when Moses could not go on without the muse a bottle could provide. A friendly guard then would smuggle in a pint of Old Grandad whiskey. No guard was named.

By the way, when I was cleaning out Forrest's house I discovered his drink of choice was Old Granddad.

Tell your story, the headshrinker said, and tell it truthfully. The truth. What is that? Some will tell you I am a stranger to truth. Old Mozzie, they will say, is nothing more than a cheap-ass con man and killer. Old Mozzie they will say would not know the truth if it climbed up his pant leg and bit his pecker. So, this is my story. I swear it is true. Though what kind of true I cannot say. My kind of true. Which, I have come to know, is in my own brain, not necessarily that of others. Sure as hell not the true of my preacherman father.

Tell your story, that balding, skinny, old fart of a doctor said that Tuesday in an Arizona Death Row cell, and it will make you feel better. Better... maybe... though I don't know why. I did what I did, so there. It happened. I felt good when I did it. Can't deny that. Sometimes I feel bad about what I done but hey I done it. Can't change that.

One time he sounded like my old man preaching to me bout the truth would set me free, but we both knew my truth will never set me free.

So this is the story of Moses Aaron Harper. Aka Mozzie, aka Robert Moore, aka Bobby McGill, aka, "the Handsome Killer."

So here I go doc. Is this what you want to know?

So my truth. I believe my father's sermons helped make me a killer. What, you may say? How can that be? You are only making excuses. Blaming that wise old man who worried so much about you, Mozzie! The man who did so much for you. He is not the one who made you such an evil worthless bastard.

Well, maybe not, but maybe so. Am I entirely to blame for me? Do not others, particularly him, hold their share of blame for me? Hell, what about God? Doesn't he? Not my GOD, Dad would say. But I suppose he and I had two different Gods.

Dad worked as a butcher for old man Hagermeister at his store on National Avenue one day a week. It was one of the many jobs he set his hand to. He worked as a coal miner in several of those old hand-dug mines north of town. He hated it down in those gassy shafts. He worked at the clay plant for a while. He dug ditches and graves. One day my mother sent me with his lunch to the old graveyard on the edge of town. There he was, waist deep in the hole, spouting bible verses and preaching at the top of his lungs. I hid behind an old willow tree and just took in the sight for a while. Who the hell was he preaching to? You never knew with my old man. Coulda been himself or the trees. Or maybe he was leaving his sermon behind in that damp hole to wait for the corpse to hear.

See, that was the only job, he always said his calling, that my Pop ever enjoyed. How many times did I hear him go on about how the spirit of God entered right straight into him as they plunged him deep in the cool waters of the Green River down in Kentucky. As soon as I come up outta that cold river and spit out the dirty water, sacred words followed right after, he would tell people. And I was but a boy of nine he would boast. He knew right then and there he was born to be a preacher of the gospel. It sure irked him when the local paper called him an un-ordained minister of some small Pentecostal church when they writing about my trial. The next day, right before they sentenced me to life, I heard him thundering at the fat reporter and telling him the only schooling a servant of the savior needed was an open Bible.

Anyway, Dad would help Hags with butchering. That old German had a twisted face that always made me look away. There was a big packing plant just over the Wabash, but Hag would not buy from them. Mine meats are the best, he would say. Not that scheiss from that Dago on 2nd Street. So, he would hire dad. Usually on a Tuesday. Hag would buy a few hogs from Aldshot or some other farmer who lived just across the Vandalia tracks north of town. Sometimes, farmers from west of town would bring in a few deer or maybe some cows to be butchered and dressed, but Hag liked his pork.

Dad sometimes took me with him in the summer. I would get a half dollar and for helping out. It was usually dad and Ezekial Washington, who was about the only colored man in town, and one of Hag's clerks who helped out. Aldshot, or whoever, would bring the hogs in about 6:00 in the morning and pen them in the alley behind the store. Washington would pull out an old rifle and take aim. He was good. A nice hole would appear right between that hog's eyes. That man never missed.

My job was to keep the fire roaring under a big old iron kettle while dad and the boys hung the carcass from a tripod so it could bleed out. Then we would all heave it into the boiling water and scrape off the hair. As pop and the men carved away I carried the hams, shanks and innards over to an old zinc tub. All the time Dad would be preaching. Knowing his audience it was almost always about drinking and sins of the flesh. Standing in the pool of blood he would rage against fornication, temptation, and the horrible outcome for the sinner who gave in to those temptations offered up by the Devil.

And then came my favorite part of butcherin' day. Hags had a daughter, about 15 then, I think. Now head on she was nothing special, just a plain-faced girl who always looked as pale as if she had just been pulled out of her sick bed. But that girl did have a chest on her. Must have gotten that from her Ma, who was a big ol' woman. Anyway, Hester was her name, she would come out to start separating the intestines and things. I would kinda sidle up behind her and watch her work. From behind that girl was something. When she bent over to drop parts in a pail; her haunches would be etched quite nicely in that worn old dress she wore when working around the store. I can still close my eyes and see that sight and think the thoughts I did then.

Later I hung in the back of the store watching her scrape out the intestines to make sausage casings. I liked the view down her dress. I liked the view down her dress. I helped her wash down the blood from table out back. You could tell she couldn't stand the smell of the blood. I didn't mind the smell at all. I gave her my best smile and tried to get her to talk. But she never took the bait. She didn't much care for me. I always had a way with the girls but she just never took to me.

The old man and I would go home after butchering. He with some money in his pockets and a bag of fresh made sausages. I had a half dollar and my thoughts.

What do you think doc. That tell you anything?

Now, our house was better than a lot of others in town, especially on the south end where we lived. Our neighborhood was filled with coal miners, clay workers or plain old laborers who couldn't afford much. There were a lot of shotgun houses or small, cheap homes built right on the ground, no foundations except for maybe a brick or two. I still remember the miner down the street and his boys spending a whole summer digging a basement for their place. Our house had indoor plumbing and a tub. Others just had the same type of zinc tub we used for the hogs at Hag's. Lots of our neighbors had a pump and an outhouse in the back yard. Ours had two floors. My parents had bought it cheap from a widow. The reason she was a widow was that her husband had shot at the guy she was foolin' around with. Trouble was, the other guy was a better shot. She sold us the house and took off for Peoria, where he had kin. Who knows, maybe something in the house made people kill.

My Dad was proud that he could provide such a nice home for his family. My Mother loved the place. She spent most of her day sweeping, dusting and mopping. I would come home and hear her singing, not the hymns

Dad made her sing on Sunday, but whatever was popular on the radio. She loved Bing Crosby and sang his songs in a very sweet voice.

I don't know, but it seemed our house was two different places. One when my father was there and the other when he wasn't. Everything could be fine and when he walked in it just all changed. Now I don't mean that he was mean or anything. Sure he would spank me or my brother and sister, but no worse than any other dad. He didn't beat us like Jack Merrill's old man beat him and his mother.

It was just like the house got darker when he came home. Like he was bringing in a black cloud with him. Least it seemed that way to me. Can't really explain it I guess. He would look at me with his witchy green eyes like he saw something bad inside me. By the time I was 13 I tried to stay away as much as I could. I took to running the streets. I loved roaming around at night. Sometimes I would find a spot and just look into other houses. See what they was up to. I liked that. Saw some pretty nasty stuff too I can tell you.

Down on 8th Street there was a house I know now was part whorehouse. A guy named Clarkston lived there. He was this big greasy looking guy. He always seemed to have a young girl there he said he was helping out cause she had no family around. But I saw them guys who would go in there. It didn't take me long to figure it out.

See it was the last house on the street. It set back against the bottom land by Sugar Creek. There was this path behind it that took you to this pond where guys would go fishing. I would sit in a batch of tall grass back there and wait. On certain nights you would see Clarkston put an old lantern out by the path. Pretty soon you would see some guy sneaking into the back yard and knocking on the door. I would wait a few minutes and then hide under the window of the bedroom. I saw quite a bit until the lights went out and heard a lot more afterwards. I was maybe 13, 14 at the time. I waited to see that lantern a good many nights until that jackass town marshal Logan run Clarkston out of town.

Now I've had my head shrunk quite a few times. From the old doc who serviced the Vigo County jail to shrinks in Indianapolis and Michigan City and on down to Tucson. While they were looking at me I was looking at them. It didn't take me long to see how interested they got when asking me about sex and fucking. Behind my back they called me a sex deviant and pervert. They think I didn't notice their crotch bulge when I talked about some things.

You too doc. Admit it.

Well I guess I might have come into manhood a little earlier than most. Who knows if I thought about sex any more than any other boy my age or not. Can't say. Don't know the answer to that one, doc. The first time I remember getting a chubby was when I was 11. Mom and dad's bedroom was across the hall from me and my little brother's. It was one of the first times I knew what that creaking sound from their bedroom was. The room would be quiet as hell except for the creak, creak squeal of the bedsprings. There weren't no moaning or groaning like I later heard at Clarkston's place. Except at the end when the old man would shout out that this was for you lord. That was my dad. He even fucked for God.

Face it. I was a good looking boy. Everyone said so. I combed my hair back kinda like Alan Ladd did in the movies. I knew the girls at school thought I was cute. I started taking some of them out to the alley behind school. A lot of them wanted to kiss me. A lot of them let me squeeze their tits too. The first one who let me do her was Hannah Cargill. Her mom and dad both worked so we went to her house. It was just off National Avenue the main street in town. I was 14. I think she was 15. Anyway she was a year ahead of me in school. She was a chubby, pimply girl. Kind of reminded me of Hester. I heard a lot of guys talk about how nervous and scared they were the first time. Not me. I just knew what to do. She said I was the first she ever let do that. I believed her then, but not later.

I also had my piano playing going for me. I am a damn good pianist. My mother played and we had an old upright at home. She played at dad's church and taught me to play. She said I was a natural and I started playing when I was seven. When dad was home we only played hymns, but the rest of the time we played what we wanted. By the time I was 17 I could play Gershwin like a pro. Later, a colored man taught me the blues and honky-tonk. I played for all the school events. When I graduated in 1935 I played piano and then had to rush up to get my diploma.

That same summer I started sneaking to Terre Haute to play with different dance bands. We told dad I was going to the movies or something so he would let me go. Back then there were bands playing all over town and I hooked on with a few whenever they needed a piano player. I played in theaters, dance halls and union parties all over that town. Even played the Mayflower room at the Terre Haute House a few times. That was big time.

It was while playing with Jumbo Irwin's band, he was a damn good sax player, that I met this colored clarinetist name Frank. He was something. He had chops I tell you. Now most bands then only had good gigs on the weekend. That was when they made their money. But Frank he knew everything and everybody. People didn't treat him like just any colored guy. They respected him. At least us musicians did. One night after we had played a big theater on Ohio Street he asked if I wanted to have some fun.

We jumped in another colored guy's car. His name was Swanee and he was a gatemouthed horn player. Now Frank was born on some sharecropper cotton farm somewhere in Mississippi or Lewsiana I forget where. But he headed to New Orleans, he always pronounced it N'awlins, when he was a kid. And to hear him tell it he done lit up Storyville. He played the clubs and whorehouses all over town. He claimed he even played with the king, Satchmo. Anyway, when he got to drinking Frank's talked even slower than normal in that syrupy voice of his. Sometimes seemed like it took him ten minutes to say a sentence.

We was sittin in the back of the car when he said "tell me sumpin ofay boy. You ever smoked reefer?' Now, I had seen the reefer movie about how you went crazy smoking it and the girls who smoked it were out for a damn good time, but had never tried it. I barely even smoked cigarettes then cause my dad hated it. He pulled out this big reefer that looked like a lumpy brown cigarette. He fired it up and passed it to me. Now boy suck it deep, I mean deep in your lungs. Damn I was swimming by the third puff. He just smiled at me and said "boy, me and ol Swanee are going to show you how to have a good time.

We rolled up to this big house on First Street. I could see the lights twinkling off the Wabash behind it. By that time I was ready for anything. It turned out to be a whorehouse just for colored folk. We went in and everyone knew Frank and Swanee. A big colored woman with bobbed hair and a tight silver spangly dress come up and asked Frank who was this little white boy he brought in. "Mozzie here is alright, Flo. I think the boy has some mulatto in him." Everyone who heard that started laughing. The biggest colored man I had ever seen come over and slapped me on the shoulder, almost falling down he was so drunk. "That true, white boy. You got some octoroon in yah?" I didn't know what the shit he was talking about so I just nodded.

Frank grabbed my shoulder and headed me to this little bar they had set up. I looked around. Every light in the place was painted red or blue. Red fuzzy wallpaper was all around the room. Frank looked at me and said "Mozzie boy. I know you got cash stuffed in those pants. Give this young man ten dollars and get us a bottle. We ended up sittin on this red divan and drinking some nasty ass rye. We had finished most of the bottle when Swanee pulled me over to an old piano in the corner. "Boy, we gonna teach you really how to play them keys." That was my first lesson in how to swing the blues. Jelly Roll an all.

After about an hour they sent me to the bar again. Finally Frank asked me if I had three dollars left. I reached in and found six one dollar bills. "Boy you are in for a treat now I'ma tellin yah." He called for Flo and had me hand her the three bucks. Pretty soon this skinny colored gal came over and took me by the hand. She was a pretty girl, about 19 I guess. Swanee said it was a good choice because she was one of them high yaller gals. Frank grabbed Flo's arm and herded us up the stairs. As we reached the top Frank grabbed me by the elbow and shoved me into a small room with a cot and washbowl on a stand in it. As I stumbled into the room I heard him telling me it was all pink on the inside.

You ever get next to a colored girl doc?

You might say that night started me on a second career. Now you got to know that in them days you couldn't swing a dead cat on the west end of Terre Haute by the river without hitting a whorehouse. It had been known as Sin City for a long time. Still is I think. The houses ranged from the cheap two-dollar whore places all the way up to Madame Brown's place on Second Street.

Now that place was something. It had plush furniture, Tiffany chandeliers and even a garden in the back. Madame Brown had a husband who was a gambler who tried his hand at bootlegging during Prohibition. He owned joints all over the place. Ma Brown was a genius at her profession. She made her girls act classy even if they weren't. She made them dress nice. You couldn't find any two dollar whores at her place. Only the best for Terre Haute's hoity-toity sinners. She advertised her place by dolling her girls up in the daytime and sending them parading through downtown Terre Haute to go shopping or pick up the mail at the post office. I've seen guys tumble out of bars, barber shops and stores just to watch them stroll by. All the time figuring what they would tell their wives so they go pay a visit to the house on Second Street.

Never made it to Madame Brown's place but I did spend many a night playing piano in some of the cheaper places. First thing they always told me was to always forget who and what you saw there when you walked back out the door. I could still name you names of the high and mighty I saw there but I won't. What I can tell you is that it taught me that all that righteous crap they try to drill in you at school, or church or elections or the radio or whatever is just that, crap. It taught me that you gotta think of you first. Screw the rest of that stuff. Don't believe it, don't trust it, to hell with others.

You couldn't beat that job. Huh doc. Music, booze and broads.

Ok, October 1939. That's when it all started for me I guess. I was playing a wedding at the country club. High falutin kind of deal. Liked those cause I could usually find someone to go home with. Usually a bridesmaid or some friend of the bride pissed that it was her good friend up there instead of her, so they tended to drown their sorrows. Like I said I was a good looking kid and that and being a musician gets a lot of interest let me tell you. That night it was the cutest little brunette I had seen in a long time. Green eyes. Just a beauty. Couldn't take her home cause she still lived with her folks. So we fooled around out in some pavilion or something out back.

Anyway. I could tell right off she was the kinda girl used to the best. But she played me kinda coy. Took me 4 phone calls to get her to come out and meet me. I was gonna take her somewhere nice. I figured I needed to go a little further with her than I did most girls. So, well, it ended with me getting caught trying to lift a necklace and watch from a jewelry store. Ended up that I got 16 months at the boys school even though I was 22 at the time. I think the old man went all preacher on the judge and they sent me there instead of state prison.

You keep asking about my first time in prison doc. Well it wasn't too bad being the boys school. I was older than most of them. I stayed to myself. Read a lot. They let me play piano in the rec hall on Saturday nights. I just hunkered down and tried to get through it. My mother came to visit me once. But it took a lot of out of her and I told her she didn't have to come back. But dad. He was there every month. Once he brought my kid brother with him. I think it was mainly to show Jeff what could happen if he turned out like his big brother. I don't think dad really came to see me. He spent most of his time preaching to the other kids. Same old shit, Follow God. Don't drink. Don't let the Satan lead you down the path of fornication. Most of the boys just laughed at him afterwards. Though one or two did take up religion.

Ok doc. Now I'm gonna get to the parts you really want to hear about.

I got out in February 1940. I had to move in back home. Everybody but my mother treated me strange. Jeff, who used to kinda look up to me, hardly anything to do with me. Dad got me a job at this canning plant outside of town. Everybody called it the mushroom factory. Isn't that a hoot. A factory for growing mushrooms. My job was, and I am not kidding, shoveling shit. The farmers around there would bring in manure to sell to the plant to grow mushrooms. Can you believe it?

After that time in jail where I was told how and when I could do something it took me a while get gat back on my feet so to say. I just felt kinda numb. Didn't drink much. Didn't chase skirt. Spent most of my time listening to the radio and picking out the tunes on mom's piano.

Then this new girl showed up at the Pearson's next door. Turned out she was Pearson's niece. Her name was Evelyn. Cute girl. I talked to her when I saw her outside. Cute girl, but kinda dumb I thought. Whenever Pearson or his wife saw her talking with me they would shoo her back in the house. But she would always give me a pretty smile when she caught my eye.

You know after all that time in jail and then being numb at home the pressure builds up. when she caught my eye.

You know after all that time in jail and then being numb at home the pressure builds up. The old man was pushing me to go into the army. Said that would give me discipline. Teach me a new way. Kept bugging the shit out of me. Hell a war was coming on. You could feel it. I didn't need to get shot at just to please the old man. I just wanted to smash his face with both my fists but that would kill mom.

So I took to slipping out coupla nights a week. Go to Brady's saloon and carry out a pint or two of whiskey. I would just sit on the grass in the back yard. No matter how cold it was. Just look at the moon and play Jazz in my head.

Now one of those nights I heard a window open. It was Evelyn. She just smiled and waved at me. The breeze pushed her nightgown around her body. She just looked at me and closed the window. Happened a coupla other times. I just closed my eyes and set there until the bottle was empty. Then went back inside.

Well doc then there come that Sunday night in April. Everybody but me went to some to-do at the Methodist church. It was a warm evening and I was sitting on the porch listening to the start of the Jack Benny Show. I had most of a pint left and was drinking it. All of a sudden Evelyn come out on her porch to put out the milk bottles. We got talking. Turned out she was alone too. The Pearsons were off visiting.

Well it got around to me saying it was a nice night for ride in the country and did she wanna go. Said it sounded nice but she was hungry so I said I would take her out to eat. I ran inside to look for the keys to the old man's car. A 35 Chevy sedan. a big back seat. Damn looked all over for the place for the keys. Turned out they were on visor in the car. Went to the diner at 4th and National. She got chili I had corned beef hash Got back in the car. She saw what was left of the pint on the floorboard. She said does that stuff really make people feel good. Some do some don't I told her. She took a slug coughed took another. Feels warm she said. I took last drink out of the bottle. No problem knew a place over in Toad Hop where could get more even on Sunday. Knew about an old mining road just south of there.

Was just getting real dark when pulled up by Sugar Creek. Still little hills of mine slag around there. Sitting car hood she had another pull on the bottle I had four. Kissing her. We both fell off hood. Laughing. Got her back seat kissing brushed back her hair more kissing everything ok til started undoing the big pink buttons on housedress she said no but wasn't going to hear that now gone too far little tramp was teasing me... little flirt.. crazy little twat. Got on top pushed inside Shit headlights coming our way.. Uncle looking for me.. gonna tell him what you did. Will be sorry.. you animal. Got up to look for car.. she got out.. scratched me. Kicked nuts ran ... Little bitch. Took whack at her.. fell. Hit her head. Lights getting closer. What shit in now.. drug her into creek car turns around. Someone else looking for necking spot. She doesn't move in creek. Fuck fuck fuck.. turned car around finished bottle. Next think am home. Go in to get coat. What to do oh shit. Take off walking end up on 150 go to Illinois hide out for while maybe go Chicago Just outside Shirkieville car pulls over. Maybe about 4 morning. Deputy smacks me hard. Knew me... got you you bastard kicks me into back seat.

Happy doc?

Didn't take them long to figure out I done it. I guess some old guy in Toad Hop heard the yelling and saw me tear out of there. He went to a neighbor who had a phone and called the sheriff. Back on 8th Street it didn't take long to figure out both the girl and me were missing. The old man saw his car was splattered with mud. One of the girls shoes was on floorboard. He called the police on me. Said he was afraid his son had sinned terribly. Someone from St. Marys said he saw some drunk heading up 150. That's how the deputy found me.

I suppose everyone says it, but I swear I thought she was 16 or 17. Would anything have changed if I had known she was only 12 or 13? Knowing me and how I think. Nah.

I hold only been in jail a day or two before the cops took me to the jail in Indianapolis. They were afraid a lynch mob would get me in Terre Haute. That happened there before. Finally they sent me back and I sat in the Vigo County Jail for months. It was right there on the Wabash. I tell you could always smell the stink off the water. Some nights I swore I could hear the piano from that whorehouse two blocks down. That was hard. Hearing someone else playing and having a good time. My lawyer made them bring in some doctor from Indianapolis. Said he was expert on criminal and deviant minds. He told the judge I was sane. Just a deviant.

My lawyer was actually not bad. A young guy. Trying to make his mark. I told my story about how she just got scared and just fell on her own. Not sure even I believed it when I said it. He said most they should get me for was involuntary manslaughter. Instead it was rape, 2nd degree murder and life. Hard time. Knew it was trouble when they called us back in. Only took the bastards 20 minutes. They had their minds made up before they was locked in jury room. It was a Friday December 5th. Two days later while I was waiting for them to take me to Indy then Michigan City I heard about Pearl Harbor on the guard's radio.

The Indiana State Prison. I was in maximum security wing. The old guards talked about when Dillinger was there. It was no boys school. Some hard cases there. I was just one of hundreds of other murderers there boy. As prisons go it was not bad some of the other guys told me. Had its own hospital, ball fields, a gym. I wasn't much for sports but took any chance I could to get out of the cell and get some air.

You asked me about how that prison changed me. Did it make me harder, I think you asked if coarsened me whatever the hell that means. How the hell should I know? I have always been myself. I can seem to fit in but it is still just me on the inside. I can con my way through things. Funny huh doc, the con man con. I got written a few times in the first years, lost some privileges but check the record my last ten years there was hardly nothing on my record. I learned what it took to get along with the guards and the other inmates.

I found out being good looking can help you on the inside same as outside. Now damn few guys inside are real pansies. They aint queers. Its just sometimes. You know fellas have needs. You seen my record. You know that early on I got cited three times for moral indecency or whatever. You know. Prisoner Harper did take prisoner such and suchs penis into his mouth. That got me in solitary for 30 days at a time. But I learned the ways. Hell you never saw where it said prisoner Harper did take guard such and suchs penis in his mouth did you. You learn things doc. Its give and take.

Why did I finally escape after serving 20 years and 5 months in prison? I guess the why is harder to answer than the how. Maybe it was because the parole board turned me down again. Maybe it hit me that I had spent about half my life in jail. Maybe I just knew I couldn't let myself die in prison. That's funny aint it doc? Now I am sure to die in prison. Ha ha on me.

As for the how I got out. Let's just say I got to spending more and more time alone with this Pentecostal minister who visited the prison. I knew what he really wanted from me the first time I saw him. I had seen that look in the eyes of so many men in the last 20 years. How about that doc. Same sort brimstone preacher as my old man. And with someone higher up in the prison bosses. Give and take doc give and take. And I got them to thinking I had already served more time than I deserved. Oh hell I laid it on thick. How sorry I was. How I was still being punished for something I did while I was a drunk kid. It just wasn't right.

So I got assigned to the prison farm. Just walked away one afternoon. There was a car waiting for me down the street. Went back to the house. Guy had a new suit waiting for me and a suitcase of clothes. The suit was a little big on me. Didn't look as sharp as I wanted to. Half hour later I was on a bus to Chicago. Had 118 bucks in suit pocket.

Long story short was hitching on 66 when just outside of Tulsa guy picked me up. Nice guy. Some sort of salesman. When he pulled over to the side of the road to take a leak I got out too. As he was hanging it out to pee I shoved him down into the ditch and jumped on him. Pushed his face down into the mud. Didn't take long. I ended up with a car, 180 bucks and a Minnesota driving license. Stole new plates off car in Oklahoma so if cops were lookin for stolen car I had different plates. See I aint never been stupid doc.

Sold the car for 300 bucks in Cimmaron and ended up in Tucson. Liked the area. Much warmer than a prison cell in Indiana. Bought myself a used tuxedo for 15 bucks and started hanging around clubs and hotels that had bands. Hooked up with this 6 piece band that needed a piano player. We had a good sound and we was making steady money. Damn, I loved playing again.

Dated this cocktail waitress for a while. Nice blonde. Stayed with her for a while but she kicked me out. Said she didn't like the way I looked at her little girl. Too bad. Had a good two years til they caught me.

So are you ready for the big answer to your big question doc? The why?

Don't know. Things just come over me. Impulses doc impulses. Couldn't shake em. Didn't try hard enough to shake em. I'd be shaving and knew had to go out and do it. Loved them didn't want to hurt them take em on a picnic, ice cream watch em smile be happy laughing never wanted hurt them really never did only that last little one got hurt she didn't see it was picnic ran said she would tell on me, just got gun from car didn't mean to hurt her had stop her or would be trouble what could I do maybe all the old mans fault all that preaching preaching preaching at me putting ideas in my head head full of sin I'd show him his constant damn preaching never let it alone he had to fuckin preach.

That's enough doc. No more. I quit.

You wanted the truth. Said I would feel better. Didn't happen. But here you got it doc. The truth about old Mozzie.

Or is it?

According to the newspapers found in the box Moses "Mozzie" Harper remained very matter-of-fact about his crimes. He received three stays of execution before dying of prostate cancer in 1972.

Constant Stranger

Indian summer had stalked the three bright days since the early frost. Like most of the older buildings, Hants Hall had a difficult time keeping pace with the weather. On this morning it chose to take up arms against the previous week's cold.

Kiernan closed his office door on the warm, clattering hallway. Hell, his office hours didn't officially begin for another fifteen minutes; no sense pushing it. Mornings were never his time of choice and it was all the worse for being a Monday. It was also Anne's late day so she and Liesl were still sleeping when he edged out the back door, scraping his head for the umpteenth time on the jagged awning.

Being midterm the natives were restless. The freshmen gathered into small, twitching clumps, sharing notes in big, nervous voices, and attempting an unworried mien with little discernible success. The few upperclassman (upperclasspersons, the new dean was irritatingly wont to call them) unable to avoid morning classes were studiously ignoring everyone.

Once again he felt himself edging toward a dark mood. Deep within was a trembling. It was barely discernible, but it was there. It was there. Small, not yet fully formed. Jagged, but sharpening and freshening. His right foot jittered under his desk, the way it sometimes did, the rhythmic way that used to cause his grandfather to ask where he was going in such a hurry.

He heard Brechmittel, East Asianist on the fast track to tenure, affected boor, one of his and Desahies' chief contenders for this year's Golden Penis award, making ready to enter the office next door. He made his usual production of it. He rattled his keys, addressed a lolling student as "young sir" in his pompous squeak of a voice, and generally pronounced to a disinterested world he was on the premises. Adam was glad he had closed his door so he was spared the "Top of the day, Mr. Kiernan," with snake's-tongue-flick of emphasis on the "mister."

He and Bob Deshaies had taken an instant, gratifying dislike to Herr Brechmittel. Bob likened him to a crab scuttling along the hallway in search of prey. Kiernan thought he resembled Peter Lorre gone fat, the later Peter Lorre of bad horror movies, not the crafty fellow who had earlier nipped at Bogie's heels. Both, however, were in perfect agreement that he was the ideal person to loathe, and made a most appropriate target for their singular brand of semi-vicious, though witty, as they assured all, brand of invective.

And there was the delicious bonus of Peter the crab's horse-faced wife. The honor went to Deshaies for having come upon her first. Kiernan knew his friend had struck gold when he sauntered up to him at the department's spring party with that look in his eye. "Grab your bridle and whip, my good fellow," Bob had chortled, "I've just had the pleasure of making the acquaintance of Frau Brechmittel... and she appears ready for the saddle."

They had fairly sprinted into the next room so Deshaies could point out his discovery. It had taken Kiernan only a second to allow that, yes, the campus was graced with a future derby winner. He congratulated his companion on his acumen. "A most suitable vehicle for equitation," Kiernan had pronounced through clenched teeth unsuccessfully suppressing a laugh. Their evening was made. They liked nothing better than to laugh when together.

Deshaies later made a stab at contrition, but failed utterly. "We are incorrigible, you know." he confessed, his long face struggling to recast itself into the iconic image of a penitent. "All part of our not inconsiderable charm," Kiernan had assured him. With that they had begun anew. Anne and Bob's wife Jill finally threatened violence to make them stop.

Kiernan looked at the pile of blue books in his briefcase; they had not graded themselves over the weekend. Another dozen or so awaited his red scrawls. He prided himself on getting them back to anxious students sooner than anyone, but he was in the mood to put them off. He reached for the soft drink on his window sill. The action allowed him to crane his neck and see the staff lot behind the university museum. His car had been joined by those of the cadaverous librarian who insisted on parking there even though the library's lot was closer and Julie's, their receptionist at the center.

The sky showed blue promise after a morning of intermittent haze, he decided as he reached for an exam. A few minutes later a windowpanesquare beam of sunlight pushed across his desk. Entrapping within its a million tiny particles. He studied them for a minute. Each followed it own frenzied orbit. No ordered, Copernican universe for them, he mused. They were swirling, without a center. Attractions, actions, reactions seemed random, unfathomable, without any reassuring force guiding them.

A hesitant hand rattled the frosted glass of his door. "Shit,'" his office hours had begun ten minutes ago. He rolled his chair across the faded tiles and grabbed for the door.

"Can, I talk to you, professor? I'm not interrupting you, I hope. I saw it was your posted hour."

Jesus, it was Wiggins. Wiggins and a Monday morning could be a deadly combination.

Only my life-- and that's instructor, one step above adjunct-- and you may if you are able-- he wanted to hiss. "No. Wiggins. Have a seat. What may I do for you?"

"I'm trying to fill out my schedule for next semester. I still have a history prereq to complete...." He paused, taking time to adjust the sleeve of his carefully chosen nondescript jacket. A pin inscribed with greek letters caught the sun. Kiernan didn't know which fraternity it was, but he was sure it was a popular one. He could never keep that crap straight.

Kiernan could feel him circling for the kill. "Well, ... even though I didn't live up to my expectations in your class, I really enjoyed it... and learned a lot. Adam wondered if his face was betraying him as it usually did, because Wiggins seemed to sense he was losing ground. "Anyway, Professor Deshaies said he thought you might be teaching 205 next time. I would sure like to get in that class."

Deshaies was a dead man. "Sorry, Wiggins, I don't know how Dr. Deshaies could make a mistake like that. I don't teach colonial. I believe Dr. Bridgemann will be offering it, as usual." That was it; the little jerk was trying to avoid Bridgemann. Dr. Benjamin Franklin Bridgemann was brilliant, the best in the department, but had been the scourge of students for three decades. The good ones endured his barely repressed scorn because they knew they were at the feet of the master; the best ones learned and later spoke of the experience in tones reminiscent of Marines who had survived the toughest DI in boot camp. The rest raced away from him faster than, as Deshaies noted, a Venetian spotting a plague ship. Maybe it was the meat cleaver tie clip he wore on exam days.

At the mention of the sepulchral spectre of Bridgemann, Wiggins wasted little time in making his exit, throwing a hurried "thanks" behind him.

Wiggins' shadow had barely cleared his office when Kiernan punched in the extension. "Asshole," he growled.

He could almost feel Deshaies laughter coming up from the floor below. "Be up in ten minutes, Big Guy," was all Bob could muster between rasps and giggles.

Kiernan returned to the exams. He dropped his pen and broke his first smile of the day. Ross, an ROTC guy who wore seed company caps and spit-shined oxfords, had done it again. In answer to a question about Napoleon's quest for empire, he posited the theory that "the frenchies followed the little corporal because he was a stand-up, take charge kind of guy and they liked him." He loved it. It was just the sort of thing Ross....

"And what's so funny?"

Kiernan eyed him with a pronounced squint. "I should not share this priceless bit of historical interpretation after this morning, but I am, as you are well aware, a fellow of charitable nature and do so hate to hold a grudge."

"Yeah, sure, you're a sweetheart. What is it?" A grin raised Deshaies' moustache so that it formed a nearly straight line under his equally straight nose and gave it the appearance of not being quite real, making it assume the aspect of a play-acting child's black tape representation of adulthood. "This has to go into my book!" Bob was always threatening to compile the definitive collection of the strangest answers ever offered up by "the bewildered student population," as he called those who "slouched through the ivy-scented corridors of academe." His last working title was How Magellan Circumsized the Globe, or Pissing My Life Away in America's Classrooms and Wondering Why I Busted My Balls to Complete Chapter Three of My Dissertation Only to be Forced to Sit Through Yet Another Bout of Intellectual Masturbation With equally Weary Colleagues. The title, he explained one night, grew out of his operating theory that the more times genitalia and bodily functions were mentioned on the cover, the better the chance he would procure a gargantuan paperback sale.

"Ross... isn't he the chubby kid with a hard-on for uniforms?" He tossed the exam back on Kiernan's desk. "What are you gonna do with that one, Perfessor?"

"I don't know. Perhaps tell him it is a bit colloquial and give him partial credit."

"Like I said, a real sweetheart. Did you by any chance receive a visit from our dear Wiggy?"

"Prick!"

"Come now, is that anyway to talk to a valued colleague-- or were you referring to young Master Wiggins?" Deshaies was more than merely pleased with himself. He pulled the chair which recently held Wiggins and his smarmy smile toward him, angled it so he could both face Kiernan and use the bookcase for an ottoman, and lit what was probably his tenth cigarette of the morning. He boasted he would smoke anything. Adam had also seen him on equally agreeable terms with nine inch cigars and a variety of pipes. Pipe-smoking-- in the days when Kiernan still indulged-- was one of the things which initially brought them together. Deshaies blew two perfect smoke rings into the sunshaft above their heads. "Still miss it, don't you?"

"My pipe, yeah. But it was time to quit, especially with Liesl."

"How is that little doll?" Deshaies claimed complete indifference to all children--even his own-- but of all his pronouncements it was the one with the most hollow toll.

"Great. She spent most of yesterday seeing just how far her natural charm would get her with her mother."

Kiernan was glad for the company. No students intruded upon them. Bob was in a talkative mood, which suited Kiernan just fine. He mainly listened as Bob filled the room with shop talk and smoke. Kiernan occasionally turned to look out his window while pretending to stretch tightened neck muscles.

"Expecting someone?" Kiernan was Caught off guard a little- especially when he returned his gaze to and saw the question in Deshaies' eyes.

"Nah, just checking the weather, I guess," he said. Trying to distance himself from the feeble words by leaning further back in his chair.

Deshaies offered sixty seconds more silence than necessary. Then, thinking better of pursuit at this time, wrenched his feet from the shelf and leaned forward. The glint brightened his eyes once more and his voice adopted a coy tone. "What's the gossip from the English Department these days? Any more closet doors opened? Any more grad assistants' doors closed discreetly?" Bob could leer with the best of them.

The English faculty, the most morally dissolute gathering of individuals since the last Borgia family picnic Kiernan liked to say, and voted the world's best living illustration of Shavian dictum by Deshaies, was one of their favorite topics. The department and its goings on provided them with hours of the most malicious fun. "Nothing definite at this point, but the discordant bells of divorce may be breaking up some of that old gang we have come to know and love."

"Don't hold back. Reveal all, my good fellow. Is it our degage Professor-Poet, that Shelley of the Middle Lands, one Hartpuhl? Please do not shatter my few remaining and speak openly of an irreparable schism between he and the faire Gwendolyn." Deshaies was in peak form for a Monday.

"I would contend he is possessed of more of a Byronic brow and temperament, though I disdain arguing the point just now," replied Adam, proud of meeting Bob's challenge, "but such is the rumor being bandied by the ill-bred amongst our brethren."

"What say they in detail? Oh, we must have the sordid detail to make our judgements. Do they speak of occurrences dark and unseemly, of deflorations and debauch?"

Kiernan leaned forward, conspiracy rising in every pore. Deshaies, too, moved so close their foreheads were almost touching. Adam looked cautiously around him. "I don't know," he said pulling back with a smile, "full disclosure has yet to be made."

Deshaies snarled, "Asshole!"

Kiernan laughed. "Honestly, I don't know the details, yet. But... I'm having lunch with BK this afternoon and all will be revealed, I am certain."

Desahies was somewhat mollified. "Okay, I know she'll come through for us. She always does." He looked at his watch and then studied the weakening sunshine to borrow some time. "Oh yeah, Jill wants to know who you had lunch with the other day," Bob said with cocked head and his best Gestapo voice, while pinching his cigarette between thumb and index finger.

Jill would, Kiernan thought, "Any clues?"

"Friday, I think. Jill said your companion was young, pretty, a touch on the exotic looking side... long hair."

"Oh... Amalia. She's one of our work study students at the Center. Has an assistantship in the Art Department, too."

"Yeah, Yeah, didn't I meet her that night I stopped by after my class... the Hebrew hippie?"

Kiernan cringed a little. He liked Amalia and didn't much care for Bob pigeonholing her like that-- especially when it was the wrong compartment into which to try to shove her. Though, he had to admit, he might have said much the same thing had he not gotten to know he so well. And Bob really didn't mean anything by it. "Amalia's a great kid. I enjoy talking to her." He hesitated a moment, knowing what he was going to say would not come out right. "She has an old soul. You can really have a great conversation with her." He enjoyed her awareness of the ridiculous in life, liked to muse about the mysteries he felt lurking behind those pretty, dark eyes.

"You know Jill, she just wondered if you ever hung around with anyone besides attractive young women." Deshaies sensed his smile was not covering his embarrassment for bringing it up.

"Tell your wife she has a suspicious nature. Most unseemly." Adam was never sure if Jill liked him. He thought she liked to blame him for playing a role in Bob's excesses. Sometimes, he was not sure if he cared for her or not, but..., "Is it my fault that discerning women are drawn to me?"

"I know, I know," Deshaies replied with relief, "women weep, and all that."

"Exactly my point."

"Jill thought it might be Kathleen. I guess she has never really seen her." Deshaies wondered why he felt compelled to add that last bit; why the hell he had not left it alone.

Kiernan asked himself why the holy hell Jill would ask about Kathleen. He didn't think she even knew Kathleen existed. "No, it wasn't Kathleen."

"Well, I promised Harve I would have the curriculum committee report to him in time for his tete-e-tete with the Dean, the bitch. I better get on it."

Deshaies was halfway out the door when he turned back, focusing his gaze on the wall above Kiernan's head, "Everything okay there, pal?"

"Sure," Kiernan replied with a shrug and knitting of incredulous brows meant to show that trouble would not dare show its dark visage, "everything's great."

Desahies showed all signs of welcoming the response. "Talk to you later," he said, disappearing into the hallway, smoke eddying in his wake.

Adam was getting a headache. He never got headaches, but lately they were coming every day. He reached into his desk for aspirin. One rolled out of his hand and under the bookcase. "Goddam it." Why was he so jittery these days? He just couldn't seem to relax anymore...

Three fingers tapped a rhythm only he could have possibly discerned, in support of harmonies known only to him. The grades on this second exam were appreciably better than the first. He wasn't sure if he was giving them too much of a break, or if they were finally catching on. Actually, he thought his lectures during the first month of the semester were better, the material more easily grappled with, but most of them didn't seem to get it. He always suspected he was easier on students as he got to know them, as Bob alleged. Was he doing them a favor by not pushing them? Maybe he should.... "Fuck it," he offered as explanation to the transom.

The sunlight weakened further still, darkening the office in tints of grey. He softened it even more by switching off the desk lamp. He pushed himself into the shadow slipcovering the corner of the room.

Deshaies knew it was Jill with the first trill of the phone. She had taken to calling him nearly every day around noon. He felt a scratch of irritation as he wondered if she were somehow checking up on him. As they talked he calculated how long it would take her to mention Adam.

"Did you ask your partner-in-crime if he and Anne could make it for dinner next week?"

My dear wife, he thought, never go into a profession where subtlety is a prerequisite. "You never mentioned anything about having them over," Deshaies said mildly, thinking it best to play the game.

"Yes, I did ... last night. Do you ever listen to anything I say?"

"I hang on every word, dearest bride." He decided he may as well have some fun.

"Right. Anyway, see if they can make it Friday." Her pause hung in the air a second too long, "Oh, did you find out who that was at lunch?"

"Yeah, I told him you were availing yourself of your inherent right as a woman to be nosey and suspicious and that he had angered your puritan soul by appearing to be having too good a time to notice you and you wished to know what the hell was going on."

"Yeah, yeah, who was it?"

"I think this falls under the need-to-know. highly classified rule," he intoned, wishing to see if he could get a rise out of her.

But Jill on the hunt was in no mood to suffer her husband. "Come on, Robert, who was it?"

"Just one of his students from the Center. A girl named Amalia. I met her once." Deshaies wished he had never mentioned Kathleen to Jill. She didn't have enough to keep herself busy these days.

A rain was coming. Kiernan could feel it lurching toward him as he crossed the street. A sentinel of the weather, like his grandfather, would have sensed it much earlier, would have deduced it from the watered sunlight washing the morning and any number of other signs. "A rain's comin', Buck," he would have said reaching up to tap his grandson's shoulder. "Look at them leaves turning up. A sure sign. It's comin'."

And so it was. The remaining leaves of the oak at the edge of the quad, the very oak once threatened by construction until an environmental sciences grad student mounted his campaign to save it by averring that it predated any white man's memory, had turned their lighter face to the shifting skies. A rain was coming.

Beneath the tree a chubby, red-faced girl hurriedly tossed pamphlets into a canvas bag. Kiernan recognized her as one of the scrubbed yet scraggly, squint-eyed disciples of Brother Ned.

Brother Ned, nee Professor Sizemore, had filled a classroom a decade or more ago-- until the not so random conjunction of his particular form of madness with the administration's insistence that he confine his blatherings to the physics lectures he was paid to deliver, and not proselytizing. When he refused, and brought Styrofoam versions of the Ten Commandment to his hearing, they had cut him free from the reins of tenure. From the classroom he had moved a few miles away to a ramshackle building that had given up its original calling as a gas station for a higher one as tabernacle. Brother Ned slapped a coat of white paint over the dust, boarded up the windows, and attached to his little cathedral a name comprised of at least seven words shouting arrogant faith and began to gather his sooted flock.

Like any fearless prophet sans honor, Ned returned to the hell from which he had emerged. Several of his days each week were spent on campus. Climbing upon a milk crate pulpit beneath the oak, he filled the air with his gentle brand of proselytism. Female students were-- more often than not is in his fevered, faith-reddened eyes-- whores, harlots, and slatterns. And were called such at the top of his vibrant voice. Male students were divided into fornicators, imbibers of evil drink, and debauched devotees of the whores, harlots, and slatterns Ned pointed out to them. For reasons unknown Ned concentrated his attentions strictly upon students. Whether this was because he considered faculty and staff beyond redemption or because he did not wish to see his pulpit snatched from beneath him was often a cause of speculation at the faculty club.

When Brother Ned, who to Kiernan's mind occasionally usurped the haggard countenance of a colporteur shuffling along the Montmartre under the weight of unsold tracts, could not make it he sent one of his sturdy minions in his stead. They would try their best, but it was not the same. The students who gathered to bait Ned did not find the sport as good with his stand-ins.

More often than not the whole unruly scene bothered Adam. He could pronounce no sympathy for either side in the seedy passion plays played out on most days. Sometimes it was the students, playing to their own form of the mob, who irritated him beyond bearing. Usually it was whomever occupied the plastic pulpit who really got to him.

On the worst days the battered brethren striving to hide their covetous glances underwent a transmorgrification, in his eyes, into the leering, clutching, tear-stained harlequins of God who conjured promethean saviours and used a tv camera as an instrument of their healing. On those days the anger would pulse through him. He would walk along restraining himself from shouting "all religion is inherently evil" to the idiot gathering. "Christians are the world's stupidest people," he once matter-of-factly confided to Deshaies as they passed the scene.

Still, he felt an involuntary pang of sympathy for the girl, coupled with a vague desire to ask her if her faith could not withstand a few of heaven's droppeths. Instead, he looked away. She probably wouldn't get it anyway.

Odd weather, he thought. This was more like a summer storm agathering. It sent out its portents. Unlike autumn drenchings which seemed to move in with the darkness to await morning wakenings, this once was announcing its intentions.

Two students slowed at his approach. Sensing they were about to speak, he dropped his head and gave them the fiercest glare he could conjure. They moved beyond him. Two steps later he heard a laugh. This is fucking Indiana, he thought, you mental defectives have never seen a tall person?

He saw Charlie from the maintenance crew hovering over the flowers and shrubs planted around the hub of walkways. His large, gentle body was doubled over. "Rain's coming, Charlie" he called out.

Charlie stood and turned, showing the grin that always accompanied him. "Hey, Adam, how you doin'? I believe you're right. Too bad we didn't get it in July."

Kiernan paused, "Lose the flowers you had left the other night?"

"No, I came back that night and covered them with straw and plastic. Saved most of 'em."

Kiernan wasn't surprised. Charlie babied his plants. He was one of the reason the campus was beginning to look like one. "Why am I not surprised by that, Charlie? You ought to make the university give you comp time."

"Slim chance of that. Especially with that sociopath I work for. Headin' for lunch?"

"Meeting a friend. You're welcome to come along." He sometimes had lunch or shared a smoke break with Charlie and some of the crew. He liked shooting the bull with them, and they were always willing to help shift things at the center without grumbling because it was for him.

"No, I can't. Thanks for the invite though. I had a quick burger. I want to work on these. Oh, hey, when will you be doing those Indian lectures again?"

"Won't do them again til next semester-- if I'm teaching US, that is. I'll let you know, save you a front row a seat."

"I'm part Cherokee, you know."

"Yeah, I remember you saying something about that. On your grandmother's side. Well... I better be gettin'," he said into a freshening wind.

Charlie grinned once more and fanned the air with a dirty hand.

For a lunch hour there were relatively few people wandering the campus. Adam usually waited for classes to begin, before venturing to the cafeteria. He was never one for crowds.

He instinctively ducked as he headed down the stairs to the cafeteria, his height appended to that natural reticence of those with poor eyesight gave him a hesitant appearance that did not seem to go with the expectations associated with people of his size.

He looked around the large room as he loaded his tray. He preferred to arrive at places first and let his companions find him. He had been victimized by his eyesight too many times and hated the feeling of being on display as he groped for his group. But he saw Bronwyn waving her hand as he stood at the cash register and his eyes strengthened at the sight of his friend.

He moved toward her. She sat surrounded by her various bags. As usual, she was laden with student's papers, any numbers of items destined for distribution to friends, and the "perfect" purse, the one he had helped her pick out.

"You look... I don't know.... tired, no.... a bit melancholy?" she said

"There's comfort in melancholy, it's as natural as the weather, in this moody sky today"

""You can cry your eyes out, 'cuz I've got a shoulder here for you; But, every day your broken heart is gonna turn a lighter shade of blue."

"Blue, here is a song for you."

They once boasted to themselves that they could carry on a quite complete two-hour conversation using nothing but lyrics from their favorite songs, but they never told anyone else, because they that it sounded as pompous as Frasier and Diane only speaking in French on Sundays. Their shared treasure of pop culture associations was quite frightening sometimes, they agreed.

"Really, how are you? I'm a touched worried by your moods lately."

He gave her the same nonchalant look issued to Deshaies earlier. "I'm fine, haven't been sleeping well recently. I'm in one of my insomnia periods."

After recounting their weekends they spoke of nothing in particular, just quaffed of their usual relaxed conversation and exchanged bemused glances at whomever had the misfortune of catching their attention. Jack Lawrence, a sociology prof, once insisted they were the most quietly vicious duo Satan ever brought together, and would only look over his glasses at them, unaccepting, when they told him it was only good, clean fun.

As the tables around them cleared, she assumed, as she called it, the gossip position. Leaning forward, eyes casting furtively about, eyebrows arched, she offered a breathy tone, "Ready for the further adventures of Phil and Gwen?"

"But of course, spare no details. I promised Bob a full and complete report, sans expurgation. He awaits expectantly."

"The dark spectral wings of divorce hover, have indeed been spoken out loud."

Adam was genuinely surprised. "You're kidding, BK. I never expected that." He had always offered the firm belief that Phillip J. Hartpuhl would never take that step. It was a truism. "No, in a perverse sort of way it is a marriage that works. It is sick, but they both get something they need from it.

"Oh, like what?"

"Well," leaning back with an affected air of omniscience, "for Phil, it is like Wilde's marriage to Constance, it gives him a structure from which to be truant. And truancy is a truly motivating aspect of his life."

"Christ," she said with a sidelong glance," you can be insufferable. I shall to stop lending you literary biographies. Though, I may concede you have a point in that regard. Pray, what does Gwendolyn gain?"

That part of the equation was more problematic, but he erected a confident front. "At first, I posit, it was adoration by association. Basking in the reflected glare emanating from the bright sun that shone from his leonine future as scholar-poet. Latterly, it has been pure martydom, the soothing balm of righteous pity naturally accrued by being married to an acknowledged asshole. She bathes in it. Gets it even though she is a well known practitioner of the art of cuckoldry-- though no doubt with good reason, in a sauce for the goose sort of way. You may recall, that upon first meeting her at your party, I suggested the air of the Bride of Christ-with-self-flagellating-whip-clutched-lovingly air about her."

She gave him a derisive "Right."

"So why is Phil thinking of seeking redress in the courts? Don't tell me it's that wino grad student who is badly in need of a clinic and three free sessions with an electrolysis?"

She raised her head in triumph. "Silly boy, it is Gwen who talks of lawyers. And by the way, that was unkind. She is really a girl with problems."

"A love for Hartpuhl being first among them. Really. Gwen?

"So she says, but you know how melodramatic she is. I would discount it at this point. She had consumed the better parts of two of my bottles of cheap wine when she told me."

"Whoa, I never really thought a divorce was possible"

"That's what you said about me and Will," she said without looking at him.

He immediately felt like a jerk, started to speak, but instead chose to notice the surroundings.

"You okay?"

"Yes…. really I am. Sometimes you just need to be called on your shit."

"Yeah."

She reached into her bag and produced copies of book and music reviews for him. They resumed their conversation until she had to leave for class.

By the time they reached the center of the quad it had begun to mist. She produced an umbrella from one of her bags. "You really alright. You seem to be having a Thoreau day"

"Do you mean I have written a hypocritical piece of treacle that will outlast me so that some day a whole generation of granola-soaked undergraduates will turn me into a secular saint and concerned, drug-soaked rock stars will fight to save my corner of the world?"

"Ah, I see once again you have donned the raiment of the King of Smartasses. I was wondering if you might be having a day of quiet desperation."

Why were people asking him that? He was acting no differently. He was sure. "No, I'm fine, just tired, that's all."

Bronwyn just looked at him.

"Actually, I was about to tell you something, but perhaps I should reconsider."

"Come on, you know you cannot stay angry with me-- or withhold vital information. As long as it is in praise of me I am all ears."

"Of course." Her face told him she was serious. "You know how I have always say you are one of my few friends that I can't find a niche for?"

"That is because I am niche-proof, as are all the great ones."

"I'm serious. I think I have a place for you. It hit me after that night we all went out for drinks at that pseudo Irish pub. You were so relaxed that night. Telling those stories from your wild days. I love listening to you when you're in one of those storytelling moods. You were as peaceful as I have ever seen you. And it hit me. You are the rebel at peace with himself." She seemed quite self-satisfied with her pronouncement.

Adam was struck by that. Pleased, but genuinely at a loss. He had never particularly thought of himself as a rebel.... Not in the Salinger, James Dean sort of way. Though he did not really see it as appropriate, he was strikingly pleased at the designation. After all, he had allowed Bronwyn to know him as completely as anyone, but Anne. She was possibly the most perceptive friend he had ever known. Still.....

"Hmmn... We'll have to talk about that sometime. You're going to be late for your class. We better go on. I'll talk to you tomorrow."

Rebel...? He did not know. He would have to think about. Of the second part of the designation, he was quite sure.

The rain had turned to splatters by the time he reached the center.

Threnody

Part, the First: Morning

Poor Old John-- his name is seldom mentioned without that rather mournful prefix-- stood on early morning sidewalks, mis-shapen head erasing the newly risen sun. The eyes that made women uneasy were cast intently downward.

He presented a sight most odd to the early traveler. One that quite often caused a slight movement of head and eye, evoked a tendril-slight spasm of pity or disgust-- at least to those unaccustomed to the scene. His outfit for this particular day was much the same as any other. It was topped by his battered pith helmet. Once white, it was now of an indeterminate color mixed of various shades of green, brown, and rust. All in all, it gave Poor Old John the look of a rather seedy retainer from one of the jungle movies from his youthful matinees. Beneath it were those brim-shadowed eyes, an amorphous nose, and a mouth given to slackness. The face was an exceptionally jowly one. Reddened folds of skin hung from his jaw to such a degree that a clerk at the drugstore likened him to the turkeys her father once raised.

The upper half of his body was encased in t-shirt. Like his headgear, it no longer resembled its original color. The uncertain combination of time and healthy doses of bleach had turned it from black to splotched gray. In addition, it showed the strain of trying to restrain John's girth; little tears and mended places were in evidence. Weight had always been a problem surrounding John. He would have been hard-pressed to recall a single day among his many decades when he was not among the heaviest of his peers. Baby fat had turned to adolescent fat, adolescent fat to a premature spread of middle age, more accumulation followed. It was just one of the many things that marked Poor Old John as different, as one on the fringe.

His trousers were of the type commonly advertised as work pants. That they were new was easily discernible by their recognizable color, a deep green. He had purchased them just last week on his trip to the larger city across the river. A thick, black belt of some plastic that aspired to leather created an artificial waistline which roughly divided the two halves of his body. The trousers were fighting a losing battle to keep the t-shirt tucked within their expanse. The hem of the pants sat about an inch above his ankles. Being taller than most, John always had difficulties finding the proper length.

Because the pant legs failed to complete their trip an unobstructed view of his footwear was allowed. Since it was summer he was shod in canvas, high-top basketball sneakers of the type once known as gym shoes. He was quite proud of them because, as he told one of the hangers-on at the drug store, they were all the style. He had seen all of the kids over at the college wearing them, he told his fashion confidante, and they called them "day-glo high-tops." His, however, were plain black and the star emblems on the sides were partially covered by his wilted white socks.

His accessories on this day were his three-pronged frog-gigger and a canvas bag to hold his discoveries. A most odd sight indeed.

John's job brought him out to move among the morning shadows; he cleans the streets. His tenure on the sidewalks had reached its twenty-third year. Except for holidays and brief declines into illness he is there six days a week, week in, week out. No one could honestly judge that he did not do his job well. Even those normally most derisive of John grudgingly concede his prowess as a gatherer of refuse. The four blocks of the somewhat grandiosely dubbed the business district are always more than presentable when he is through with his patrol.

John came to his vocation because his hometown had the misfortune of being on the wrong side of a turgid river opposite a much larger city. Despite this, the merchants had always been able to make a go of their concerns against the competition of their larger brethren across the bridge-- until the Eisenhower years. It was then that the new-fangled shopping centers, as Wilson the shoe man, called them, began to gnaw away at their trade.

Hometown customers found it more exciting to take their dollars to the newer, bigger stores. The businessmen in John's hometown had always been a fiercely independent lot. Their concerns ran to their enterprises and no one else's, but even they began to see that banding together might be of benefit and formed a merchants association to stem the flow.

One of their decisions was to find someone to make downtown more attractive, to "gussy it up," as Wangelin the grocer put it. It was Mr. Ford, the druggist, who broached John as the candidate for sweeping the street. Ford, a man of legendary kindness given to "accidently" forgetting to send bills to his more wanting clients, always kept a weather eye out for John, having respected John's mother. It took some persuasion on his part to convince the table full of doubters, but the job was offered to John at twenty dollars a week. It had been his ever since. No one but John knew that June 16, 1978 would mark his tenth year on the job.

The morning had paraded much like the thousands of others. As always, he had begun in front of the diner's window proclaiming the "Hearty Home Cooking" to be tasted behind it. From there he lumbered off in search of the discarded. Upon spying something he launched his gig at it, brought it up to eye level for investigation, and then tossed it into his bag. The procedure was repeated unerringly along the street. Reaching the boundary of his territory, he made his usual pause to survey the path behind him.

Much had changed. The merchant's association had held its own for the first few years, but then the mall came. After that, the decline had begun with a vengeance. Now the empty stores were threatening to outnumber those still holding on. Nearly every other storefront presented a dusty plate glass window seemingly held together by a spiderweb of tape and children's scrawls. John, however, was not looking at the decay. He was searching for someone to talk with.

Talking to people was one of the supreme joys of his life. He would strike up a conversation with any one at any time, about anything. He was always disappointed when whomever he engaged in conversation invariably had to hurry off to other tasks. Today, no such opportunity had presented itself;

the morning was still a bit young for many people to be on the streets. More than a bit discouraged, he emptied the contents of his bag into the barrel standing guard on the corner and crossed the pocked road.

Turning east, he moved out in search of more game. Thirty minutes into the return journey the eyes that made women uneasy spied something. Practiced eyes told him it was not the customary candy wrapper or crumpled religious tract. He shifted the gig to his left hand, using it as a support. Bending stiffly, he retrieved folded pages. Straightening himself with some effort he pulled them to within inches of his moist face. He studied them with the assiduity of an archaeologist intent upon some strange hieroglyphs until now unknown. A look of triumph, almost exultation, washed across his mobile features. It was a letter, apparently from one sister to another. This treasure was not consigned to his bag to lie with the flotsam; instead, he placed it almost tenderly into his back pocket. He would save it to read at home. His steps became more brisk.

He neared the end of his duties. People were starting to filter into his area. Storeowners, clerks, and early shoppers moved grudgingly through the sunshine to take their places for the day. John greeted each one within hailing distance, which for him could be several blocks. A few gave more than a quick, mumbled reply or awkward gesture, but most seemed to discover they were suddenly tardy.

Later, Mrs. Reedy paused to say a word or two. She was one who always stopped to spend a minute or so with him, to enquire about his health, or notice the weather. She had been a student of John's mother-- and besides it was the Christian thing to do. Mrs. Reedy prided herself on her upholding of the Christian Way. She asked him to carry a box from her car into her notions store when he got a chance. Always eager to please, John told he would get right on it. He liked to feel needed and he knew she would openly slip him a dollar.

He softly sang a hymn as he continued his meander along the rest of his route; Whispering Hope trailed behind him.

When the last piece of trash had been removed, he looked behind him once more to see a straggle of arriving toilers and a customer or two scattered along the sidewalks. Two men shuffled out of the diner into the cocoon of their automobile, paying John no notice. Already, a few of them had left a trail of paper behind them.

Restless as always when the job was done, John prowled the alley behind the stores. He was not really seeking anything, just looking. A row of mostly white houses, their backs turned toward the stores, formed an uneven line. Few had been standing when John was a child. Then, the area was mainly open field as it was the last section of town to develop.

It was not until the good people fled from the flood of miners who encamped on the north side to burrow in the last of the mines (a lot of them had been dark-skinned-skinned, Italians or bohunks, they were called) that houses had begun to spring up here. They were among the last built in the little town, and that was forty years or more ago. As John had reminded Billy Simpson just the other day, no one had built a new house in town since Charlie Fedder's boy built that two-storey job fifteen years ago on Milton Street.

Had John been in one of his contemplative moods-- and he was much more given to pondering than most would credit-- he would have mused again how he had seen nearly every day of those houses' lives. That was a favorite topic of his when people gathered evenings at the drug store. If allowed, he would recite a biography of any of the structures to those strung along the fountain counter. On such nights he would not allow himself to be swayed from their stories. Neither the ebb and flow of customers, nor the continual diminution of his audience would distract him from his narration.

But this being Friday, his day on the town, he had much to do and little inclination to philosophize.

Seeing several boxes stacked behind the Tropic Isle tanning Salon reminded him of his promise to Mrs. Reedy. He slapped himself on the head with the exaggerated motion of a third-rate comedian miming forgetfulness and muttered as he went off to see to the errand.

The notions store already held several browsers when John pushed his way through the door. In an effort to keep up with the times Mrs. Reedy had added a line of craft items and renamed it the Ginger Cat. It had yet to be discovered by the cognoscenti across the river and the change had done little to boost sales. The locals still mainly referred to it as the notions store.

Hearing the bell announce an arrival, Mrs. Reedy looked up, her Christianity failing to conceal a grimace. "I wonder what he thinks back doors are for?" she breathed to her assistant. She knew how quickly the shop would empty if John tarried too long.

John, for his part, adopted his courtly manner for the occasion, dropping the box and doffing his hat to the first woman he encountered. It was one of his three ways for dealing with women. The other two were to occasionally place a hand on their back and speak in a confidential tone-- a rare occurrence-- or simply pretend they were not there. Cat-quick smiles and a general lowering of eyes greeted him as he moved to the back of the shop. Following John to the storeroom, Mrs. Reedy's expression told everyone he would soon be gone. Inside the storeroom, she told him to feel free to use the backdoor, it was closer. In his pocket as he departed were two new dollar bills. Afterwards, it occurred to Reedy that she did not know why she had given him the extra dollar.

"They say his mother wore her corsets too tight when she was carrying him. Back in them days even married teachers weren't supposed to be pregnant," she explained to her assistant's rolling eyes.

It was Jordan Clinton's week to pay for the street cleaning. For that reason John spent more time than usual looking for someone to pass a few minutes with. Normally he rushed to collect his earnings so that he might ready himself for his outing. But dealing with Clinton disturbed him.

Clinton had purchased the drug store from Mr. Ford several years earlier. It was the third "pharmacy" in what he liked to call his "holdings." The verdict passed on the newcomer by most of the townspeople was that he was a little too slick for his own good. Changes had been made. As with his other stores he had retained the old name, thinking it good for business. Mr. Ford's good name and the soda counter were about the only things to remain as before. Clinton closed charge accounts that had carried many through rough stretches. He posted the names of those who offended his dignity by writing a check with funds insufficient to meet their obligation, and added a "spicy" section to the magazine rack. That last decision had upset many, particularly Brother Swann from the Assembly of God Church down the street.

Clinton, however, had ignored the brief storm, pointing out to all who would listen that sales were brisk. The fact that his was the only drug store left in town had not harmed his cause. Still, most customers admitted that it was just not the same.

Another of Clinton's changes had been moving John's payday to Friday. He confided to his store manager that it was partly because it was his day in the store, and he liked to twist the knife a little in the old fool when he paid him.

Knowing that he could wait no longer or he might miss his bus to town, John walked reluctantly to the rear door of the store. He lightly pressed the button of the service bell Clinton had installed and peered through the wire reinforced glass. He could see his boss ostentatiously rip a check from the pad; he could also see the vipersmile slither across the druggist's face.

As was his custom, Clinton asked John the reason for his visit. He was rewarded with John's squirm and mumble about "Gettin' paid." Clinton was too busy to carry through with his usual routine of enquiring about John's tailor or his big plans for the money. Instead, he simply held out the check in such a way that John had to reach awkwardly forward to grasp it. Just as John's fingers touched it, Clinton tightened his grip momentarily. He held John with his eyes for a few seconds and then released the check

119

with a laugh. As John turned to leave he heard Clinton tell some unseen person that if he paid the old fool what he was worth he would starve.

John moved along the alley before turning north toward mainstreet. It gave him an inch or two of breathing space, a bit of time to shake off the scratched feeling that overcame him when his dignity was affronted. Whenever embarrassment clouded him he felt a heat rise from his neck and a veil of rushing sounds cloak his ears. It was a condition which might last a few minutes, or hours that stretched into topored days. Today it lasted only as long as it took him to spy the Reverend Duss.

The Reverend Duss was also a man to be found outside the boundaries. Increasingly, he had become more admired by those resolutely choosing to remain outside the church's carved door than the faithful who took their place inside upon the highly polished pews. Many in the peace-aspiring congregation of the Harmony Methodist Church were worried about their leader. He had become the main topic of the hushed discourse among those who gathered in Fellowship Hall on Wednesday nights to steer the course of the church.

Most agreed that his first twelve years as their pastor had shown him to be the steady, level-headed man they had hired him to be. The changes in him, some said, had begun over a decade ago. Mrs. Reedy, always a self-avowed scholar of nuance, postulated that it was the death of his son in the boating accident that began the reworking of the man. Floyd Donnerman, a physician without the healing touch, believed the cancer that engulfed Duss' wife of twenty years had also burrowed into the minister. Others just shook their heads.

If they could come to no mutual understanding of the causes of the change, they all agreed upon the first outward sign, his growing of that beard. A rich, grey-flecked growth had appeared along the outline of his jaw. Without a moustache, it gave him the look of an Amish farmer, or a retributive biblical patriarch come to them in the flesh. It unsettled not a small number of the faithful.

They became further disenchanted by what they saw as his increasingly odd behavior over the years. Next, it was the change in his sermons. The comforting traditional harangues against agreed-upon sins or in support of long-perceived virtues had taken on decidedly moralistic undertones. His calls for the feeding of the hungering halfway around the world or diversion of monies from the mortgage fund to establish a day-care center had led to a squirming of bodies and a turning of heads in the pews ranked below him. He had also become involved in politics. Even during his suppers in their homes he guided conversation toward things that interested him. More than one host later complained of being lectured about nuclear weapons or prejudice over the roast beef and glazed carrots. All in all, according to long-time deacon Harry Siddons, Duss had become "damn preachy."

Not one of the congregation had yet to bring up why the church had been lit for all the world to see at 2:00 AM last Tuesday morning. The man had performed a wedding of two women from the north side, it was whispered.

John, a member of the church for about as long as any, saw no great problem with his minister. He had long considered Duss one of his special friends. The Reverend had presided over the burial of John's mother, even though she had disdained the comforts of the church in her last years. Until Mrs. Duss' illness had moved with sodden, steady treads into its final months the couple had made certain John sat at their table at least once a month. John, then, would brook no criticism of his friend from anyone. "He's good people," he would tell anyone who pressed the subject, "ain't changed a bit."

As Duss moved toward him, John found a mail box to lean upon.

"Good morning, John. I see you have completed your labors for the morning. And another fine job of it, from all appearances."

John, whose pride in his work was unlimited, smiled deeply. "Mornin' Reverend. Yep, finished up about an hour ago. How about you? Finished that sermon yet?"

John's familiarity with his habits always surprised Duss. It usually struck him most forcefully on those days when he ran into John four or five times. "Bright and early this morning."

As he turned to head home, John wondered why Duss no longer carried his Bible.

John's house was three blocks from mainstreet. Appropriately, it too presented a most odd sight to the passerby. Two stories, with a wrap-around wooden porch, it was two years older than its occupant. The color scheme was the first thing to attract the eye. For most of its first half century or so, it had presented a wholly white face to the world. That lasted until John decided that a bright yellow paint was to be the agent of a much needed change. In exchange for an afternoon's work cleaning the storeroom at the hardware store, he received six gallons of a mixture styled as Canary #2. This luminescent shade in itself would have been no great cause for alarm; it was the manner of application that led to neighborly hushed discussion.

John's easily felt terror of heights did not allow him to climb more than three rungs up a ladder. As a sad result, Canary #2 swathed the house only to a height of slightly more than nine feet. Above it a twenty year-old coat of white paint chipped and fell haphazardly to earth. The chips gravity had pulled from the clapboards now outnumbered their brethren who remained. It was especially barren around the second storey window in what had been John's mother's room. So darkened and weathered were the boards that Mrs. Lemieux's grandson had, as she proudly related, dubbed it the house with the black eye. John had steadfastly refused the generosity of those neighbors who offered to paint the rest of the house. He was picky about people bothering his place. Latterly, he had added a black trim which had elicited little comment from a jaded neighborhood.

He deposited the tools of his trade just inside the front hallway and moved across into the parlor-- his mother had considered the term living room vulgar-- to the stairway. He removed the letter from his pocket and placed it gently on the table by the stairs. The climb was growing no easier. He had to grasp the bannister with both hands to conquer the last few steps.

There were two very distinct worlds in John's house, with the stairway acting as the border. He ventured onto the second floor. The top floor was travelled to only in the daytime. It was comprised of the room he had lived in most of his younger life, the room in which his mother sewed or graded papers, and two barren rooms that had never really fulfilled any capacity.

He no longer used his old room. It was only the site of the clothes press that held his good clothes within cedar-lined walls. There was no bed, no table. The rocking chair had long since been carried away. Tan wallpaper rampant with fading, though still strident eagles stilled in flight clung gingerly to the walls. Tumbleweeds of dust were stirred by his tread. Selecting the outfit for his excursion, he retreated down the stairs. The descent was quicker than the climb.

He glanced at the clock on the table. Calculating that he had time enough for a nap and quick change before catching the bus, he shuffled into his bedroom.

Interlude

It had been his lucky day. The minutes before the bus' arrival were usually tinged with some trepidation for John. He worried over the status of his preferred seat and who the driver might be. But today, everything was working out just fine. He had his throne, the first seat behind the driver, the one perpendicular to the others, the one that allowed him to talk to those on either side or opposite of him without straining or twisting. It had the additional advantage of making it virtually impossible for those around him to ignore him or pretend not to notice his presence.

His favorite driver was behind the wheel. Ed Tyson was always prepared to chat with his riders. Twenty years of following the same path had given him skin like parchment and no little insight into the human condition. He early on judged John to be harmless and more than a trifle lonely. He no longer bantered with the old guy out of obligation, but, almost without realizing it, had grown to like him.

The other drivers who sometimes spelled Ed on the route were not known to feel that way. The wiry, bald man carried a sign that curtly told all and sundry the driver did not wish conversation. The woman driver was hard to figure out. Some days she would talk and joke with John; on other occasions she kept her eyes on the road and her mind to herself. The worst was the young guy who played with his moustache. John had heard one of the women call him Phil.

But this ride had been a pleasant one. He talked with Ed and even got the woman three seats away to mumble replies to his questions.

John stepped from the bus two blocks south of the city's main street. It was another of his habits. Even he was not sure why he got off short of his destination. Perhaps so people he later encountered might think him a resident of the city-- or at least the owner of an automobile.

Part, the Second: Afternoon

Poor Old John in his more formal attire was no less an arresting sight than in any other of his raiment. The pith helmet's place had been taken by a brown fedora ornamented with a thin silk band and a yellowed feather. It did not quite complement his sport coat.

The jacket was loden green, except for the steak of white on the right sleeve, the result of a failed attempt at stain removal. It covered a shirt of a color that would have been familiar to anyone who served in the military. A sort of olive drab, it was covered by an eccentric pattern of what appeared to be Fleur-de-lis compressed into the shape of an egg. A tie that have been produced from the same pigments as Canary #2 grew down from the folds beneath his neck.

One again his slacks failed to complete their journey to the tops of his shoes. This was their first trip to town. He had scarce believed his great good fortune in finding a pair of sixty dollar slacks on sale for only fifteen. The salesman had proclaimed their green and tan plaid as equally suitable for clubhouse and the links. John had knowingly nodded as he handed over the cash. Well worn wing-tips clarified the origin of down-at-the-heels.

Draped upon the sleek body of a known trendsetter the ensemble might have been looked upon as daringly fashionable, but on John it did not call out for such acclaim.

He headed out, moving over streets he did not have to clean, noting each bit of trash he passed.

His first stop was the big bank on mainstreet. There was a branch in John's hometown, but he made it a point to save a transaction for his trip.

He always felt himself transported into a larger, more teeming world when he entered the limestone monument to its founder's business acumen and disregard of others. John had always marveled at the huge main room. As a child he made certain that each footfall landed in a different white or black square. The expanse of polished marble and brass continued to gleam as they had on his first visit. The indecipherable letters and numbers that chased one another across the screen at the back of the room were no more fathomable today than in the past.

He did not pause to seek out a familiar face before heading to a teller's window. The ensemble of solicitous faces changed with such relentless regularity that even John no longer tried to keep track. He was pleased to find himself standing before a kind-faced young women with red hair. As she bent forward to take his slip he noticed the freckled cleavage chastely presented above the button of her white blouse.

At first she seemed a little taken aback by the multi-hued creature appearing at her window and seemed reluctant to speak. John, however, had acquired a few stratagems over the years which often enabled him to squeeze out a bit of conversation. One of the most reliable was to enquire about an item of clothing or jewelry. It did not always succeed, but today it had garnered him a two-minute relationship and the history of a silver broach. He airily left the bank with the crisply new bills he always requested folded neatly in his pocket.

From the bank he ambled along the first leg of his trek. No store window went unstudied; even the empty ones drew his scrutiny. None, however enticed him inside. It was a stretch of ladies' shoe stores, furniture emporiums, and jewelry shops. None held any real interest for John and served only as objects upon which to exercise his curiosity.

Fran Karkovice, who travelled to work each day from John's hometown, had spent seventeen years amid grease and murmuring voices. The boundaries of her work world were defined by the twenty-two foot lunch counter she patrolled from ten to two-thirty, five days a week. Hers was the last of the many five-and-dimes that once stood within three blocks of each other. The counter she was careful to wipe clean was the last of its kind in the city.

Mostly, she enjoyed her work. Over the years most of the faces had become familiar-- if not always welcome. Howard from the bank was, as always, sitting on the third stool, the one that afforded the best view of all those entering the store. She had not cared for him at first, it being against her better instincts to trust a rich man, but she had found reason to think kindly toward him for some years now. And it was not just because he had called off the dogs when Kerry had been laid off from the box plant and the mortgage payment never seemed to find its way to Howard's bank on time.

Marie from Frohmeyer's Department store chattered away with Beth from the card shop, both subsisting on salads this week, though neither really believed it would help much. Jack Jimison, so quiet and courtly that no stranger would guess he was a beer salesman, silently read an out of town newspaper. Four lawyers grumbled to each other in the corner booth. Fran was glad booths were outside of her station.

She glanced at the front door just in time to see John edge his way into the store.

John had ever thought variety stores the nearly perfect mercantile vehicles. His mother sometimes brought him to such wonderlands during childhood summers. He loved wandering up the stacked aisles imagining the uses to which he would put each of the many splendid items. On those glorious days when his behavior the previous week had allowed him a purchase he would nearly fret himself to death trying to decide what to take home.

As he sidled up the center aisle a sideways glance told him there was no open seat at the counter. Never mind, he would explore among the wares until a place opened up.

He floated a greeting to a thin woman named Nina, calling her by name. She looked up from a ziggurat of yarn and nodded. She was new and John had only seem her twice before, but he was pleased that a name tag allowed him to personalize their relationship. He paused at the greeting cards, ignored the plastic flora growing from a table, and settled into the record department. It was his habit to familiarize himself with the latest releases, as they were called. He never purchased any, indeed, seldom listened to music. He did, however, like to keep up with things. He liked to know what people were talking about in the overheard conversations. Satisfied that he was now abreast of musical trends, he walked to the book racks, all the while checking the counter.

Books were important to John. He read two or three, sometimes more, a week. Monday was his library day, and a book or two was often the only booty he carried home from his trips to town. His tastes were somewhat eclectic, and would have surprised many. He tended toward nonfiction, especially books about World war II and the Old West. Those subjects also dominated the novels he favored. Not just any fiction would do. He would not accept the contrived violence and sex that often stared at him from the paper covers. In westerns, it had to be Grey or L'Amour. James Jones was preferred above all others in the pursuit of martial themes. His secret pleasure was the work of Grace Livingston Hill, a long dead romance novelist once favored by his mother. Her old fashioned tales of romance were as stiffly chaste as a Baptist maiden when compared to the rows of heaving bodices that faced him, but they touched with each reading.

He noticed the exodus from the counter brought on by the passing of the quarter-hour and headed for a vacant seat. He tried to appear casual, but when it looked like new claimants pushed through the door he noticeably quickened his pace. The result was his wheezy greeting to Fran.

"How's the soup business?"

"'Bout the same John. How are you today?"

"Purty good. purty good. It's a little warm out there today."

Olivia, a waitress most aptly described as a harridan, and the self-styled "Queen of the Booths," slid Fran a look of amused pity that said "That's what you counter people get."

John spent no little time studying the clouded menu, finally choosing the beef manhattan. It was quite nearly the perfect meal to him. Over the years he had made himself into a quite acceptable cook, but smooth mashed potatoes had always proven beyond his talents. He turned to survey the surroundings as Fran angled away with his order. The nearest customer sat three stools beyond conversation range. She was a death-pale woman so thin as to suggest a recent hospital stay. A carefully untended mass of red hair cascaded-- erupted might be more suggestive-- around her thin face. A BLT and a paperback whose contents could only have been unleashed by continuous ingestion of a hallucinogen shared her attention. She was known as Meg, or that hippie girl, depending upon whom was asked to identify her.

She made it a point of honor to lunch here at least twice a week. Each visit left her wallowing in a rather sublime feeling, as she described it to her diary. She was proud of her ability to both mix with everyman and still feel so apart from it all, a sojourner walking an enlightened path. She seemed not to notice that the path became less crowded with each passing year. Sometimes she chatted with John, told him of the healthiest foodstuffs or little known, but enabling, beliefs. Today, she chose silence.

He nodded or spoke to all who passed to the cash register. His meal disappeared quickly. Fran occasionally stopped to speak a common tongue. When John mentioned he had seen her ex-daughter-in-law she found a spill to be wiped at the other end of the formica. A reconciliation was concluded over the cash register and he sent his best to Kerry. After he left she found three quarters resting inside the ring left by his plate.

Sated, John resumed his rounds. He spent the next hour in what could only be described as an extended dawdle. Again, store windows were inspected, merchandise appraised, nods offered up to all with the unstinting generosity of the saint. He meandered quite contentedly through afternoon shadows occasionally softened by the appearance of a stray fleet of small clouds.

Sidestepping crates of soda bottles, he plunged into the cigar store with all stops out full. He bellowed hellos to Frank and Don, the brothers who owned the place. His rasp echoed along the long, narrow room as he made sure Laban, wrapped around a pool cue in the back, knew John had made it in.

The Conestoga Cigar Store and Snooker Parlour was a darkened relic only vaguely aware of its role as an anachronism. It still afforded Frank and Don, grandsons of the original proprietor, a comfortable existence. Cool and dark no matter the season, it continued to offer refuge and solace to its discerning clientele. Bootleg liquor, a man's vote, a sportsman's intuition, and a woman's sloping, perfumed breasts had been among the commodities bought and sold within its mirrored walls.

A good cigar, John would tell people, was a pleasure he had cultivated through the years. He bought three Garcia Y Vegas on each trip. While Frank dug into the mahogany and glass case John chatted with Claude, still known as the shoeshine boy even though well into his seventh decade. Their in-depth dissection of the weather was terminated by the arrival of the fat insurance man who appreciated the high shine only Claude gave his shoes. John, not one to bother a man at his work, turned to appreciatively inspect the pictures of Don's grandchildren, He spent the next half hour watching the pool games; he never acquired the skill himself, but had come to an appreciation of its artistry. He laughed heartily at each joke and eyed the restroom door. Being a man of extreme modesty, John would not visit just any public facility. Too, he thought such occasions should be an entirely private matter. For those reasons he always chose to use the empty facility, invariably a spick and span place, at the Conestoga before leaving.

A failing brown brick building marked the eastern terminus of John's journey. The old-timers knew it as the old Big Four Depot. For those who knew only the hegemony of the automobile, it was simply the tattered building for which no use could be found. For a time there had been talk of turning it into a restaurant or a collection of shops, but nothing had come of it. Now, the remnant of the railroad and the city argued over who was responsible for interring the remains. Meanwhile, bricks fell, windows became targets, and the trains that once stopped now fled past on rusting rails.

John-- this being one of the rare occasions when he allowed himself to defy constituted authority-- ignored the admonishments against trespass and struggled up a small concrete and sharded glass hill. With his most determined tread he made for the rear of the old station. Below the crumbling platform a pile of discarded tires from the service station next door offered themselves as a bench. Invitation accepted, John leaned against the platform and ceremoniously lit a cigar.

The Big Four Depot was as much a part of John's myth-legend-being as Styx to Achilles or the tantalizing, seemingly-reachable sun to Icarus. It crystallized his childhood, helped give shape to his life, acted as a definer of identity. His memories of the place were at once dim and hopelessly aggrandized; he recalled each in its turn. Each visit afforded an opalescent veil of solace and regret.

John's father had been a railroader; his real name was Ferris, but everyone but his wife knew him as Hutch, for reasons unclear. He started as a stoker, but his affinity for machinery was recognized early on. In time, he was named foreman of the repair shop, despite his avowed admiration for Gene Debs.

By the dawn of John's memory Hutch had taken on the role of travelling troubleshooter. He would hop onto a train with his tools close to hand go to the side of an idled machine. For this reason John's mind was early filled with scenes of comings and goings.

Hutch was known as the best of men. A letter found much later among John's mother's possession, but until that time unremarked upon, had confirmed this aspect of his father to John. Written by one of Hutch's "boys," it told of his concern for his men. It described him as a good boss, "a man always willing to help out." Apparently the writer was unaware of the irony folded into the phrase.

The philopsophe who muses upon the role of the unseen hand or the random conjunction of people places and time would find much to conjecture about in this part of John's tale. How different might all have been, they could say, if Hutch had been a more selfish man or the editor of the local paper a man of a less finely honed sense of the absurd.

Any flights of fancy notwithstanding, the story was a plain one. John's father, returning from a trip to Mattoon, Illinois, was about to head home when he noticed one of his men at work on the undercarriage of a freight car parked alongside the platform against which John now reclined. There was uncertainty about what sort of repair the young man was attempting. All that was really ascertained later was that he requested Hutch's expertise and, upon inspection, Hutch had sent him off to fetch a tool. That was how Hutch came to be kneeling beneath the platform when the wheel of a cart loaded with sewing machines found the edge and toppled its load onto his back.

Two blocks away, the editor was informed of the story. Knowing it would be the type of tale to interest his readers, he decreed the story be given prominent display on the front page. He composed the headline himself: "Local Man Slain By Sewing Machine."

That headline had done much to give John an early identity. He quickly became known as the son of the man killed by the sewing machine, or the boy whose father died by the hand of Mr. Singer. It was used by other children with the built-in predilection to taunt. It echoed from the lips of adults he passed on the street. To all but a very few it summed him up, or was seen as an adequate description. Whether used as eulogy or epithet, it stung with the same ferocity. Even when he did not hear the words, but only saw the look, his neck would heat and his step quicken.

Thus, every return to the station began as a sepulchral visitation, though the somber tone seldom lasted long. John soon latched onto more comfortable thoughts. He was wont to recall to a select few listeners the time his father smuggled him onto one of the trains during a repair trip. John would spin an elaborate tale of a friendly engineer enlisted as co-conspirator, of a midnight sprint under a glistening moon, and sweeping through a running wind. Whether the story was true or not was eminently beside the point. John was no longer sure if it was as he remembered, or whether it might have been a story related by his mother, or if he had read it somewhere and taken it deep within himself. It was the part of the apocrypha of his life. True or not, it soothed.

Perhaps the reason he had never chosen to examine it too closely, to offer it up under the brightest lights, was that it was one of the few recollections of his father he could summon forth. He was only eight at the time of the accident. Before mainly consisted of images random and mainly unfocused. He still felt strong hands lifting him into a tree's branches. Sometimes, on the eddies, he saw a face fringed in grey that was never as stern as the one in the picture at his grandfather's house. Of course, there were the scenes of his father leaving for work. He could particularly picture the sight of Hutch's back, could summon up the sharp angles of shoulder blades pushing out of bib overalls. Though few, the collected impressions buoyed, lifted him on the scend of a wave.

He shifted himself, wiggled his legs, raised his arms. If he was not careful the flow of reminiscence would become a hemorrhage. He would then be forced to relive the slow walk behind the horse-drawn hearse with the ornate script on frosted glass. Once again, he would wonder why his mother never cried, or why the person most solicitous of his feelings was the man from the mortuary.

The man, possessed of the name of Will and a pair of pale blue eyes that said his work would not harden him, had talked to John whenever opportunity presented. Towards evening he had taken John home with him for supper, singsonging his way along an elmed street. Afterwards, Will stopped to talk with John every time he came across him. More than half a century later John still felt ashamed for not going to the man's own funeral. He had wanted to go, wanted to tell Will's five daughters what a kindness had meant, but could not bring himself to do so.

The service now complete, he raised himself from his seat and headed for the street, walking slowly away from his shadow.

Back upon the sidewalk his pace quickened. The emergence from reverie usually imparted some urgency to his steps, as did the Berdache Lounge which loomed ahead.

The Berdache was one of the few remaining bars on a street once illuminated by their raucous light. John had never been comfortable around taverns of any kind, or saloons as he called them still, but the Berdache was the worst of all. Its neon-tinged habitues were the type had been warned of as a child. Those kind of men, the ones to watch out for, the ones who put their hands on you. John had never actually had any sort of contact with such a person, but he knew they were to be avoided. As always, he hardened his gaze and pointed it straight ahead of him.

A choreographer unlikely enough to be walking the same streets might find John's perambulations of some interest. Like one of their creations, John's movements could be quite telling if studied by the practiced eye. His body was often the corporeal manifestation of some inner toil. The turn of his head, a spasm of a hand, even the pace which seemed to undergo periodic modulation, could be seen as the physical expression of thought or motion. A gaze fixed or eye averted might be seen as welling discomfort or a tendril of hope. Perhaps the twitch of fingers meant thwarted desire.

They could mean anything. But most of all the passing danseuse might remark upon John's pace and offer that it told the tale. Like a yet wordless child John often used movement as an expression of desire. Also like a child the same movement might carry several meanings within it. A slow pace could indicate reluctance fascination, a quicker one anticipation or flight.

The Berdache always gave a boost to his step as he passed. Robert from the church, who in earlier days sometimes walked the streets with John, before he shuffled the halls of the nursing home, had taken notice of the phenomenon years before. Upon reflection, he once told his wife, it seemed like one of those Thurber cartoons in which the inanimate takes life. He could almost see the building assume a human form and reach out a soiled hand to give John a nudge along his way. Metaphysical nudge or not, something always pushed John quickly past the block long parking lot and beyond the music store and vacant bank building.

His step did not slow until he approached the blue building that acted as one boundary for an empty lot returned to an uncertain nature.

The bricks of The Gentleman's Retreat had surrounded Greek Jimmy's candy store for thirty years after their placing. Their natural hue had first been despoiled by succeeding coatings of whitewash in the fifties after a Mr. Phipps had turned the building into a record shop. Phipps, vaguely recalled as a man who played in several local dance bands before the war, had decided to turn his musical energies in a new direction with the advent of rock and roll.

With four thousand of his third wife's dollars he opened a store that sold record players, sheet music, and the wailings of those he did not pretend to understand. The business prospered for over a decade, thanks to an ever changing pantheon of sweetly menacing troubadours and coyly manufactured talent. Mr. Phipps even became something of a hero to many when he defended the music and its ardent listeners against the efforts of a service station owner and a Southern Baptist preacher out to protect their hometown from yet another bad influence. Hell, he once confided to his monied spouse over dinner, it was no different than that darkie stuff he used to hear in New Orleans.

Phipps closed the store in 1969 when he could no longer ignore the siren call of a January sun and moved to Florida. The structure did not long stand empty.

The Gentleman's Retreat quietly made its appearance in the uneasy summer that followed. Its birth was made possible by one of those periodic spasms of quasi-honesty when a few people admitted sex existed in thought, word, and deed. Its midwife was a sociology professor at a local university. The youngish scholar, given to wearing patched jeans on his lanky legs and any current cause celebre on his ennobled sleeve, told all who would listen that he was merely taking advantage of the growing openness to free man from the clutches of his own taboos. To do so he offered the soothing ministrations of volumes filled with nude women clad in leather and men of frenzied mien clutching one another. Both sexes were chastely covered by clear plastic wrappers.

The town's first adult bookstore became the target of scattered protests, one led by the selfsame minister who had earlier tried to warn all that this was where rock and roll would lead, but the store's success proved the strongest desires were the secret ones.

The young academician profited in many ways. Desires turned into quarters, which changed to dollars, which filled the hand-tooled wallet lovingly crafted by one of his students. He was scrupulous in tithing five percent of the profits to ever hovering causes. In a burst of inspiration he decided to conduct his class on human sexuality amid the plastic women and artfully produced genitalia of his bazaar. The incident elicited the Warholian fame he had anticipated. Many offers were made; two were accepted. One was from the president of an ivy-walled university, the other from the lawyer of a certain man from Detroit wishing to purchase the Retreat.

The new owner, like druggist Clinton, retained the name but changed the bricks to robin's egg blue. The same paint was used to cover most of the windows when local authorities decreed the harlot's face was to be covered lest those who did not wish to see it should happen to catch a glimpse. Advertising posters were pulled from the glass and paint obscured the view to a height of six feet. Only the determined would be allowed to succumb to its blandishments.

The Retreat usually pulled John into its orbit, invariably slowed his newly invigorated step. Almost always he found a reason to halt completely. On this day he fumbled for something lost in his pockets.

He had visited the store, but never in the daylight. Years before, when the buses still ran till nine o'clock one night a week, he had made three fevered trips into its garish light. Each had been planned in advance. He had stayed in town long after his usual departure time. He ate a nervous supper in the cafe around the corner. As darkness settled he took his place on a cold bus bench offering a view of the well-visited back door. To the passerby he was just awaiting the bus. When traffic through the door had slowed and he felt no watching eyes he made his move. He scurried through the heavy door. Each time he waited just inside until the eyes that made women uneasy adjusted to the light. He stood perfectly still, not wishing to accidently brush against anyone and give rise to unseemly suspicion.

The first time he waited a long while before venturing further, standing a full five minutes listening to projectors clatter and doors squeak. Finally, he moved onto the checkerboard floor out front. The sights astounded him. Instinctively, he veered away from the paraphernalia that covered one wall and concentrated on the magazines adorned by smiling women. He spent an hour looking; the heat rising within him. A dozen times one hand snaked toward the racks while the other reached for his wallet, but he left without a purchase.

His second visit was shortened by the appearance of a delicate looking woman in her twenties. Her frank proposal of temporary companionship so stunned him he was outside before he realized he had not drawn breath for many moments.

In a way his third visit was prompted by the second. The next week he arrived at the same time. He wandered the store for half an hour, half in fear, half in hope. The wan young woman did not show. When the clerk asked for the third time if he needed anything, John slipped into a booth to watch a disintegrating film purporting to show a man and two women enjoying themselves.

He also made his one and only transaction. He escaped through the back door with a sack of magazines clutched hard beneath his winter coat. Defying any logic, he kept the magazines hidden deep within the closet of a house to which no one ever came. From time to time, always late at night, always with a glance over his shoulder into the shadows, he would pull them out. Eventually, one Sunday before church, he wrapped them inside several layers of newspaper and tossed them into a trash barrel blocks from his house.

John had not been inside the store since. The buses no longer ran late and he could not walk through the daylight to its door. He looked each time though. His height allowed him to see over the paint but he saw little. His vision did not permit a clear picture of what was for sale, though he knew what was there.

His fumbling produced the second of his cigars. He unwrapped it as he walked on.

Interlude

Upon the steps of the war memorial the old men gathered, backs turned to the lowering sun. Silent, stiff, faded, they huddled close together, as if seeking the comfort of a fire. Their eyes, made opaque by age or loss, occasionally peered onto the afternoon streets. They were a fixture. To many of those hurrying by they were as much a part of the urban terrain as the fierce statues made of iron and rust and another day's truths. A ragamuffin group if he ever saw one was the verdict of the maddeningly thin county clerk who could see them from his window.

They may have been edge-tattered, but in its own way their conclave was as exclusive as any in town. There was no real logic as to who was accepted and who was shouldered from the circle. Military service was often a requirement, though not always. Sometimes it was a shared outlook, probably molded by loss. Sometimes it was some perceived gift that added to the coterie's sense of itself. Sometimes there was really no reason.

The last member added was younger than most by half. Jimmy Wayne's war had been under a tropic sun. He was from John's little hometown. John had known Jimmy Wayne's father, a man who had returned from his war with a fifty percent disability and a taste for idleness. Jimmy Wayne had happened upon the group one October. At first, most of the group had given him no more notice than the blowing leaves that followed him up the steps. Eventually, a kinship was perceived by one, who brought the rest to his vision. Jimmy Wayne's tenure had not been without its difficulties. He was banished from time to time for sauntering up with his hip flask full--or worse-- half full. Such behavior was not countenanced-- except for Harlan Jeffcoat. After Okinawa, they all agreed, Harlan was entitled.

John's price of admission had been the death of his uncle, Jonathan Hauptfeld. John carried his mother's brother's name. His uncle appeared on a plane only slightly below his father in John's pantheon. Jonathan had chased after the colors shortly after an enraged America declared itself tired of the Kaiser and his minions. He left his studies at the Normal school before the end of his third year, but his education and abilities had been good enough to make him an eager young officer.

His war was seemingly a good one. His letters to his sister carried not a hint of the life spent in an open air charnel house. Instead of marching home in 1918, Jonathan found himself guarding supplies in Mother Russia. The fellow who had been untouched by the yellow clouds of gas, or German steel, or the hundred diseases which settled around him, died when he fell through a hole planted in a Russian lake by the first touch of Spring.

John stepped easily into the gathering, a hello for all. He pulled the remaining cigar from his pocket and gave it to Omar Cooper, his first friend in the group. He and Omar and Kitman and the rest did not talk about much of anything. The weather, the politicians scurrying through the building behind them, and the news printed that morning all were commented upon. Their voices were stilled only when a passerby drifted too close to their domain. But the discourse would soon continue. John was sorry when time came to head for his bus.

Upon the steps of the war memorial the remaining old men gathered, blending with the metal beings, postured, immortal, fading.
Part, the Third: Evening

Poor Old John, returned to home and nourished of the companionship of his fellows, walked toward a shallow sun. He wore his third change of clothes of the day. Actually, he was at his most presentable. His buff plaid shirt blended nicely with khaki slacks long enough to graze his cordovan shoes. His cap, salt and pepper tweed, old, lived in, could almost be described as jauntily perched upon his head. The sidewalks he had cleaned in the morning were once again the resting place for wrappers, cans, and anything else which fell prey to gravity and uncaring hands.

After supper he had wandered back down to Ford's Drugstore. He knew Jordan Clinton would be long gone on a Friday night. John did not enjoy the Friday night downtown as much as he once did. In years past it had always been a busy place. The door at Ford's was seldom long unopened as customers hurried to pick up potato chips or quarts of the exotic ice creams Mr. Ford so enjoyed eating or recommending. You could always count on people filling the booths and stools along the fountain. Back then there were always a dozen conversations ricocheting off the big mirrors along the back wall, making themselves available to any ear caring to listen.

It was considerably quieter now. Rarely were there more than three or four people in the store at any one time. The few who did come in seldom tarried longer than necessary to pick up a prescription or magazine. Usually the only loungers were teenagers sporting tattered denim and a world weariness that seemed to weigh heavily upon them.

Not like the old days, John often thought, when they were brighter, cleaner, and used to crowd out the older folks after basketball games. Rarely long discouraged by the inevitable loss, they would sweep in wearing their sweaters and saddle shoes, pegged pants and letterman sweaters. John recalled them as nicer and more fun to be around. Not like these new ones who scared him a little. He didn't feel sorry for them, he mentioned to Billy Simpson before leaving, their problems were no worse than those other teenagers he remembered.

John turned for home at the branch library, rather deftly sidestepping twin seven-year olds on pink bicycles. If their parents had been sitting on the porch he might have stopped to talk with the little ones, but he had learned it was best not to pay too much attention to children if no one was seemingly around. People did not trust the way they used to. Instead, he just waved and advised them to watch out for cars as he walked through the shadow of the Harrington's house.

It was getting dark enough for the streetlights to blink on, but they had yet to show much effect. On evenings like this people sat on plastic, metal, or wooden chairs, or sprawled across swings and ledges. Escaping the heat or the reruns, their voices mingled with the flitting of millers and the buzz of mosquitoes, and were sometimes punctuated by a snore or two. Occasionally the unthinking would raise their voices to a level that invited attention, but not too often. Most who lived on this street had the wisdom to confine any disagreements to the interior. Children were watched, neighbors visited, the lives of others quietly examined with an eye toward improvement.

John's neighborhood had held up better than most in the struggling town. A city council member lived just up the block, so any needed sidewalk or street repairs were usually made with some alacrity. John's neighbors were mainly older and not so much affected by the layoffs and plant closings headlined across the river. Most of the husbands on his street had seniority or secure positions. Though not rich by anyone's standards, most could look forward with comfort. They took care of their places and pointed to those who didn't. The councilman made sure his neighborhood was zoned to prevent mobile homes, or trailers as he called them.

At the corner of Arthur Street, John crossed to his side of the block. He always crossed at the corners. He was not sure why, but he always made sure he came to a complete stop and looked for traffic. As usual, he slowed in front of the green house, second from the corner, to make certain all seemed normal at the Murphy place. Old Murph had been dead for ten years now and his daughter Vi lived there with her husband and youngest grandchild.

John had worked for Murph for nearly thirty-five years. When he first started Vi must have been about ten, a gangly little redhead who would slip into the store in search of a ginger beer and one of the coney dogs Morgan the butcher made up each day. It was a great game to her, a piece of high adventure. She would peek her head through the loading dock door and ask John where her Poppy was. Then the conspiracy would begin in earnest. At least twice a week Murph would saunter through at just that time and John would have to hold a cautionary finger to his mouth and scurry Vi behind the hand truck loaded with potatoes or canned goods. When the coast was clear John would shepherd the giggling girl to the little room off the meat locker where the treasure was waiting. Vi would raise the soda bottle, wink mischief at John, and slyly drawl. "I guess we fooled Poppy again." John would aver that indeed they had, but cautioned care for the next time.

Those adventures usually capped John's day at the IGA. Actually, his shift normally ended at 2:30, but he always waited for VI. The old IGA was at the corner of Tenth and Main, now just a block beyond the terminus of John's cleaning territory. He had done a little of everything. Mostly stocking and cleaning, but in a pinch he would help the meatcutters or, in later days, run a cash register.

Murph was always after him to get into the meatcutter's union, but John knew it was not the trade for him. He would arrive at 5:30 and help unload deliveries when not cleaning. At 7:00 he and Murph would join Morgan and Alice, the bookkeeper, for coffee. The rest of his day was busy with running in and out, talking to all the customers, and trying to keep up with his boss. Occasionally, Murph sent him out on a delivery. In the afternoon the two of them would edge toward the back to keep an eye out for Vi.

John worked for Vi's husband Jerry after he bought Murph out. Jerry was a fine fellow, but when he built the new store out on the highway, John took his leave and a small pension. He did not blame Jerry; it was the right thing to do. Jerry and Vi invited him over from time to time, but he seldom accepted. They always sent a card on his birthday and a ham at Christmas. In return John would shovel the blanketed walk when Jerry was without time and always kept an eye out for Murph's little girl.

To prolong the evening John decided to watch the lightning bugs dance from his porch. He ignored the swing and pulled the clam shell chair from the corner. Made of metal, it always received a fresh coat of paint in the spring. On nights like this he would pull it close enough to use the porch rail as a footrest and peer at the universe around him.

John's house had been built by his grandfather. He remembered the old man as standing ramrod straight with a shock of fair hair drooping over a perpetually closed right eye that made him look as if he was forever winking at the world. He had changed his name from Willem to Edward when he reached the United States. Edward after a sailor he had met on the trip from Le Havre to New Orleans, he would tell John, sometimes on this very porch. He had arrived in St. Louis to broadsides declaring for Lincoln of Illinois. He only stayed in the bustling city for a few months. Too much, too much, was the only explanation he offered to the cousin with whom he lived.

Having long been a swimmer against the current, he defied convention and headed east, settling in a small town in Illinois with an eye to buying a good piece of land. He had only been there a few months when he accepted an offer to go to war as the substitute for the son of a local lawyer. He did not really need the money. He came from a respectable family of burgers

142

in Germany and had migrated out of desire, not need. Still, it was a chance for adventure.

Keeping out fifty dollars and depositing the rest, he set out with ears pricked for the sound of the drum. Somewhere in southern Maryland, he thought, a projectile launched by an oak tree rent by a cannonball pierced his right eye. An army surgeon pulled the splinter out the next day, but the sight had already escaped. It was not something he seemed to let bother him. Because of it, he would say, he had met Lincoln himself while recuperating. Returning from the war Edward saw a piece of land he wanted, a fringe of prairie that seemed to beckon him. It was made perfect in his eye when he found it straddled the state lines of Illinois and Indiana. He liked the idea of owning acres in two of the states for which he had fought.

Edward enjoyed a modest prosperity. He joined in the odd small venture from time to time, owning pieces of a small mill, dry goods store, and a miner's saloon in the prairie village six miles to the east. But mostly he worked his farm; each spring savoring the taste of a pinch of his soil. He married late in life, but not too late to father four children. The third child, and only girl, was John's mother. To his regret, though not vocally so, none of his children felt the tug of the fields. Each looked to paths that took them away from the farm. Admiring their courage to seek their own ways, Edward gave each a purse filled with the price of 160 of his acres.

The two oldest boys, reversing their father's trend, went to California, where they ended up working for the same bank. Their visits home came before John's memory, except for the three days after the old man's burying. The youngest son, the one Edward most hoped would stay to walk his fields, had made the old man happy when he reported in a letter home that he had come within twenty miles of his father's birthplace. That was just a few months before he sailed for Archangel. The leavetaking of John's mother had been most difficult for her father, partly because it came within a year after his wife's death.

John could recall most of his grandfather's visits. The old fellow, despite nine decades, would clatter up the porch steps, grab a wayward wisp of his grandson's hair, and gently steer him to the bench. He was usually in town to transact some business. They would talk. John heard of Mr. Lincoln and crops. Edward heard of boyish things. Occasionally, the times John liked best, Edward would talk only to him. He would leave John with the admonition to tell his mother that his grandfather was there.

The chattering of the crickets finally usurped the voices of children on the next block and the muted reverberations of the TV across the street. A heavy quiet mixed with the blue night. Soon, John's porch light was the only one pushing shadows onto the sidewalk. "Time to go in," he said to no one.

Inside the door, carefully locked, he kicked off his shoes and loosened his belt. Opening the mirrored closet door, he exchanged the loafers for a pair of carpet slippers so old they immediately became a part of his feet. There was no need to fumble for a light switch. Every lamp and chandelier had been blazing since his departure earlier in the evening.

The stillness filling the house seemed so right, so just, he did not reach for the tv knob. He glanced from the clock on the table, which read 10:47, to the one on the mantle, where it was always 11:00. The ornate hands of the mantle clock had not moved for nearly two decades, but it could not be consigned to the darkness of the attic above or suffer the ignominy of the trash barrel out back. His father had brought it back from one of his runs to Chicago. Hutch was known to sometimes browse antiques stores and curio shops. Most of his finds had not passed his wife's muster and were invariably given to neighbors or handed over to one of his men.

This one, however, had found a home, first in the glass fronted china cabinet. John had moved it to the mantle a few days after his mother's death. Hutch had made the purchase for the simple reason that he liked the look of it. He only knew it was called a pillar and scroll clock and had been made sometime before his father-in-law's war. John had little more information. Once, at the library, he had run across a picture of a similar clock. The book said it was made in a factory belonging to Eli Terry of Connecticut. That was not the name on Hutch's clock, but it did not really matter. Nor did it matter that it served no function other than ornamentation. John liked the pastoral scene executed beneath the ornate face. He was wont to lose himself in the hillocks and rim of maples that became New England to him.

"Besides," he liked to tell Vi, "it was right twice a day. Which was more than he could say about most people."

Looking around, John grabbed a small red volume from the bookcase, though he knew it to be a dangerous choice. He lost himself in the platform rocker and pulled close the ottoman with the time-rubbed jacquard covering to support his much travelled legs. Instinctively, his fattened fingers traced the Marine emblem stamped upon the cover. The map inside the front cover portrayed an area as recognizable to him as his own streets. Lunga Point and Henderson Field need not have been visited to be remembered. The Tenaru and Matanikau were more real and exotic to him than the brown river he crossed every week.

As always, he paused to gaze at the defiant eagle grasping a stylized book in the same talons that clutched the arrow and the branch. The experience was always made more palpable by the Publisher's forthright assertion that the book had been "manufactured under wartime conditions" and did not squander valuable paper. He had seized Guadalcanal Diary the very day it appeared on the shelves of the little bookstore up from campus. Because Lucy was with him he had hidden it under his coat. He read the book at least twice a year since, and held it much more often.

It was not difficult for him to feel the terror of a jungle filled with a treacherous yellow enemy known for its stealth and the cruelty of a raging Comanche. His hair would still sometimes bristle as he thought of crouching in a rotting foxhole that played host also to slithering, gleaming snakes and primordial smells. He could just as readily imagine the jaunty camaraderie of men trading japes about an enemy seldom seen, and griping about officers, and food tasting of pestilence.

Although he had not served, the Marines and their little hells were John's war. He followed it every day of it in the papers and traced its progress on maps culled from his mother's old textbooks. He was always the most knowledgeable of those who gathered in Murph's aisles to discuss the morning's war news or what Mr. Heater had said the night before on the radio. He haunted theaters in search of newsreels. He marveled twenty times at how Preston Foster and William Bendix had brought his favorite book to life. But, as he came to realize, he had never really considered fighting any of those battles himself. Enlistment never once crossed his mind.

It was not as if his 4-F status had come as a relief. He would have served; he harbored no doubts about that. It was that he just felt another fate awaiting. He simply never thought he would ever don a uniform. Strangely, it was his mother who had closed tight her eyes and breathed deeply when he told her of the draft board's verdict upon him.

Her reaction had surprised him. Their relationship had always been somewhat troublesome. In the twelve years since he had moved out on his own, the thirteen since his semester's failing, his returns to his mother's house had been brief and covered with a dust of obligation. That day he had been dropping off her grocery order-- Murphy always insisted John make the delivery-- on his way home to Lucy. He and his mother had even less to talk about since he had taken up with Lucy.

He had used the classification only as a vehicle for conversation. After all, he was at the upper end of the age bracket, fat, and not universally perceived as the martial type. And, he never expected the call. But his mother must have succumbed to dark thought. Her vision had obviously carried beyond his. After the news she had quite literally sunk into the chair he now occupied and looked beyond her son. Before he left, she had reached up to adjust the collar on his jacket.

He still, twenty-three years after her death, sometimes attempted to form a more complete picture of her. He had tried and tried.

She had married his father late and was thirty-two when John was born. In a day when few women dared, she had gone to college, well, the small normal school in town. She had taken her share of the money old Edward gave his children and bought with it an education and some sort of affirmation for herself. It had cost her $185.00 a year, room and board at a nice place included.

His mother was not one to reminisce with him, but he knew from eavesdropping on conversations with her friend Eleanor that her school years were cherished. When cleaning out her papers, John had come across some old school programs and pamphlets. She had belonged to a literary society and the drama club. In her senior year she read a convocation poem about the "Fields Beyond Campus Streets" and played Desdemona in the auditorium.

John only knew that his parents met on the old interurban. His mother had been teaching at the secondary for eight years when Hutch had finally called up enough nerve to speak to her. She was returning from a play at her alma mater, he going home after another run. Hutch once told Edward he had been noticing her for months, but thought her unapproachable until noticing one of her shoe strings was untied.

Most thought it an odd match for either to make. Ellen would have been considered bookish even if she were not a teacher. She was known to read Shakespeare and rumored to speak some French. Hutch was seldom seen reading anything save Zane Grey and the idol Debs' union paper. Hutch was a voluble man, offering words as freely as a zealot his faith. Ellen was thought dour even outside her classroom, and given to a silence that could drown out any strident voice. The husband recognized no rank. There was no man better than he, certainly none any worse. The wife was proud of her profession and her standing. She carried on her life with the formality of a minister's smile.

What drew his parents together John did not know. Of the strength of their bond he could not guess. He remembered no shouts, no curses flung against the moonlight painting the walls. No long ago tastes of real bitterness washed across his palate. Certainly, he recalled no rages, no fits of anger or contempt. The kind Lucy told him about and refused to reenact in any way. Neither was he able to summon any great store of less virulent emotions. If the house provided by his grandfather was not an angry one, it was also not one of joy.

Why he was his mother's disappointment was, too, beyond ken. Dozens of times over her last six months he had pushed himself to ask, but never filled himself with enough strength. He was not that stupid; both of then knew that. He could have read and understood most of the same books as she. He could reach for higher thoughts. He was an awkward child possessed of little grace, but that was something any mother could overlook, he thought. His failures were no worse than anyone else's.

The only times he ever wished to shout so loud that even she would hear him were when his father died, and it did not pause her stride, and after Lucy, when her eyes would not hide the pleasure of a prophesy fulfilled. Once more, when she sent Eleanor to ask him to come back home. Still once more, when she had turned away before closing her eyes.

Around these bare-boned facts and miasmata of memory he had tried, for some few years, to provide some flesh and gristle so that he might make some semblance of her. To them he added her curious turn from Austen and Dickens to romance novels and the renting of the silence to which she had once abandoned his father. Though, he noted, she always referred to him Hutch as "your father" without allowing him the dignity of a name and usually talked of the skills rather than the man. John had talked to Eleanor, but she was forthcoming with little but assurances that her friend was a good woman of strength and character.

The phrases, bright but hollow as a bell without tongue, had little helped. After death, she had remained the ghost she had been before. But, finally, she did not haunt.

He closed the book on Col. Edson talking about Tulagi. He rubbed his eyes and looked around the room. The eyes that made women uneasy fell upon the letter on the table. He had nearly forgotten. Gently lifting it from the shining maple, he returned to the rocker and ran a smoothing hand over the two pages.

The contents, written in a sloping left hand, were unexceptional. It was a letter that might be described as chatty, from Helen to Jessica. Helen lived in North Carolina and related scattered bits of her last few weeks. She told her sister of her niece's dancing lessons and her nephew's baseball games. Brad's job was going well and she was still working part-time for the realtor who had sold them their house. Jessica could expect visitors for the holidays and new pictures of the kids would follow. The letter ended with greetings for all and assurances of affection.

He refolded the letter and tucked it between the pages of the book. He was weary enough for bed. He fetched his gigger and canvas pouch from the front hall and carried them to the back porch. He folded the pouch and placed it on the green bench. The gigger was placed against the wall, its tines turned upward so as not to be dulled by the concrete. He was, after all, Hutch's son.

The day's final ritual followed. After putting his clothes on the chair he pulled on crimson pajamas. In the bathroom he washed his face with the hard, square soap and brushed his teeth with salt water. He pulled back the quilt that was always on the bed. He arranged the three pillows carefully. It was a warm night, but not an uncomfortable one. The old bed creaked its acceptance of his bulk for another night.

Interlude

Lucy arrived, as always, accompanied by the chorus of the minnesinger. She looked as she had in that first glance that became a vision. A halo of black, black, black hair framing that small face. A wisp or two fell upon the white skin of her forehead, another brushed the collar of her red coat. Above a retrouusse nose were grey eyes that looked wide open even in moments of repose; when she was excited they seemed to jump out at the one lucky enough to stare into them. Long clouds of cool breath jetted from lips not quite full.

It was easy to see the strength in her small body. He could feel it in the touch of her fingers that became orphans when cupped within his. He could taste it on the downward curve of her calves, could trace it in the valley between her breasts, could sense it in her abandon. Anyone could hear it in the voice that refused to shout.

She came to him with a husband in the war and her thoughts in a place he could never divine. During their seventeen months and twelve days he came to know the nuance of her moods, the depth of her needs, but her thoughts too often baffled. Why he was chosen was never to be understood. When he asked, she who could be so articulate, only asked in return if he was glad they found each other. John had no desire to tempt fate.

She trembled there beside him. On cold nights only her small face, more childlike than womanly, would peek out from beneath the quilt. She could not get close enough to him. Her smell was there; she never wore colognes, but produced her own fragrance. Sweet, tangy, a saltiness, that touched the crisp sheets. It took years of washing them to prevent the aroma from torturing him.

She was .... gone.

Without noticing it, John had heeded the advice of an unheard fifteenth-century de'ploration to clothe himself in mourning and weep great tears from his eyes. She must have made her decision early on. She probably had known it the night he asked her if she ever thought she loved the wrong man, the night after she learned Frank was being shipped stateside.

"No," in a voice without waver," but I have thought it possible to love two at once."

It was not the answer he sought. She seldom gave the answers he wished.

"I don't," he pushed at her. "I think there can only be one love."

"I know. I also know you are not one to accept its inequality."

She was gone.

Three weeks later she left. She left them both. She was strong that way. She did not look back.

She was gone. She left him bereft, fragile, raw. He did not understand.

John did not know how Frank dealt with the loss. For his part, John set about to systematically eliminate all the physical traces she left behind, all that was her to him. It took him years. Clothes, combs, pictures, a forgotten red glove, were all discarded. He did it without hatred; rancor was never an emotion he associated with her. Sometimes he did it out of despair. Twice, after he had touched two other women, he did it out of respect. He did it to make it easier, though he did not view it as cowardice. He did not do it because he wished not to think of her, of how it might have all been different.

The book, for some reason, was the last embodiment of her left in his life.

Part, the Fourth: Netherland

Poor Old John, dressed in crimson, at home in his bed, tired from his journey, switched off the light. The eyes that made women uneasy closed on the moonlight around him. He settled himself in. He slept a sleep of some peace.